Eighth Grade

Other titles in The American Teen Writer Series:

Published by Merlyn's Pen, Inc.
4 King Street
P.O. Box 1058
East Greenwich, Rhode Island 02818-0964

Printed in the United States of America.

These are works of fiction. All characters and events portrayed in this book are fictional, and any resemblance to real people or incidents is purely coincidental.

Cover design by Alan Greco Design.
Cover illustration by Andrew Laws. Copyright ©1996.

Library of Congress Cataloging-in-Publication Data

Eighth grade : stories of friendship, passage, and discovery by eighth grade writers / edited by Christine Lord.
    p.   cm. -- (The American teen writers series)
    Contents: The clubhouse / Ryan Tate -- Cricket song / Catherine Pickut -- Beneath a dark mountain / Jessica Hekman -- A day at the mall / Mark Harris -- My father / Sarah Orvis -- In defense of Hades / Sarah-Scott Brett -- The mission / Ben Miller -- The questing beast / Matthew Roessing -- It rained for Stevie / Jodi Zislis -- Starry night / Matthew Cheney -- The chief inspector / Katherine Stanley -- Theft / Elizabeth Webster.
    ISBN 1-886427-08-9
    1. Short stories, American. 2. Youths' writings, American. [1. Short stories. 2. Youths' writings.]   I. Lord, Christine. II. Series.
PZ5.E34376
[Fic]--dc20
                                                              96-27806
                                                                 CIP
                                                                  AC

99 98 97   6 5 4 3 2

Eighth Grade

STORIES OF FRIENDSHIP, PASSAGE, AND DISCOVERY
BY EIGHTH GRADE WRITERS

Edited by
Christine Lord

The American Teen Writer Series
Editor: R. James Stahl

Merlyn's Pen, Inc.
East Greenwich, Rhode Island

Acknowledgments

Jo-Ann Langseth, copy editor, is gratefully acknowledged for her significant work in preparing these manuscripts for original publication in *Merlyn's Pen: The National Magazines of Student Writing.*

The American Teen Writer Series

Young adult literature. What does it mean to you?

Classic titles like *Lord of the Flies* or *Of Mice and Men*—books written by adults, for adult readers, that also are studied extensively in high schools?

Books written for teenagers by adult writers admired by teens—like Gary Paulsen, Norma Klein, Paul Zindel?

Shelves and shelves of popular paperbacks about perfect, untroubled, blemish-free kids?

Titles like *I Was a Teenage Vampire*? *Lunch Hour of the Living Dead*?

The term "young adult literature" is used to describe a range of exciting literature, but it has never accounted for the stories, poetry, and nonfiction actually written by young adults. African American literature is written by African Americans. Native American stories are penned by Native Americans. The Women's Literature aisle is stocked with books by women. Where are the young adult writers in young adult literature?

Teen authors tell their own stories in *Merlyn's Pen: The National Magazines of Student Writing*. Back in 1985 the magazine began giving young writers a place for their most compelling work. Seeds were planted. Now, the American Teen Writer Series brings us the bountiful, rich fruit of their labors.

Older readers might be tempted to speak of these authors as potential writers, the great talents of tomorrow. We say: Don't. Their talent is alive and present. Their work is here and now.

About the Author Profiles:

The editors of the American Teen Writer Series have decided to reprint the author profiles as they appeared in *Merlyn's Pen* when the authors' works were first published. Our purpose is to reflect the writers' school backgrounds and interests at the time they wrote these stories.

Contents

How Randall became a Rat: A tale with a tail.

The Clubhouse

by RYAN TATE

The sound of sneakers thumpity-thumping filled the air as the five of us raced violently for our beloved clubhouse. Being together felt different today, though, because of new blood in the Rat Pack. His name was Randall, and his initiation adventure was just commencing. As we scrambled up the frayed rope ladder like the Rats we were, the bright Saturday sun shone vividly through the east window.

"If we don't put a shade on that window soon, I'm gonna go blind like that geezbag Smithers," Bobby exclaimed.

"Who's Smithers?" Randall inquired.

"The old dork who lives in that shack," Joe answered with his arm extended in a northerly direction.

"Yeah, he's blind as a bat and more ugly! Do you remember the time we T.P.'d his house? He didn't notice until he found the piles of pulp in his gutter! And even then he thought it was just dogwood petals!"

Elmo said.

The whole tree house shook with cheery chuckles. Our Rat Pack meeting had begun like all the others. Bobby, Elmo, and Joe were all hunched over their home-made pinball game, while Randall was still investigating his new surroundings. I, on the other hand, was in the corner working on some graffiti with a black marker. Joe glanced in my direction.

"Twink, you rodent! What are you writing now?" Joe screamed.

I stepped back to reveal my work. It was a drawing of the ugliest face my hand could manage, and next to it were the words, "GIRLS STINK."

"Oh yeah, girls stink. Tell me something I don't already know, Twink. Now get over here! Bobby just hit the bottle cap on our pinball game and I think he might get the new clubhouse high score. You too, Randy," Joe said.

The four of us cheered Bobby on, but he still fell two hundred points short.

"Ha! You dweeb! My score is unbeatable!" Elmo gloated.

"Oh, shut up, or I'll tell everybody about your little incident with Mrs. Foster and her German shepherd," Bobby retaliated.

"OK, I'm cool," Elmo quickly replied.

Joe took charge and said, "Now, Rats, it's time to get down to business."

Everyone except Randall deposited twenty-five cents into a small Pac-Man bank and sat back down. Digging deep, I found a dirty quarter next to a couple of candy wrappers and reluctantly plunked it in. I noticed a peculiar glare upon Randall's long face. He seemed overwhelmed by all the excitement.

Joe stared at his hand and continued, "Now, I have our agenda in my hand, uh, I mean, on my hand, and it says that all we have to do is initiate Randy and then we can party! Do you think you lamebrains can handle that? Randy, prepare to become an official member of the Rat Pack!"

One by one we marched off to Elmo's house while I brought up the rear. We burst in the front door and headed straight for the refrigerator. I seized the ketchup and handed it to Bobby.

Elmo began, "The first step in becoming a Rat is taking a nice big swig from an ice-cold bottle of Heinz."

Randall grimaced and took the bottle in hand. As the container touched his puckered lips, we could all smell the salty stench of the crimson concoction. I sensed an air of uncertainty: Randall looked like he wasn't sure he wanted to play our game. He must have been reminding himself that it was just a tiny mouthful, but it didn't seem to help. His eyes glazed, as big as dinner plates. The blood-red material sluggishly made its way down the neck of the frosty bottle. Slowly, the thick substance slid to the back of his mouth. Randall swallowed as quickly as he could without gagging. He cried for a glass of water to no avail—we were all in hysterics!

"One down and two to go!" I exclaimed with a loud cry.

"This next one is a whole lot easier. All you have to do is eat a fly," Bobby stated.

"Uh, no thanks, guys. I'm already full from that delicious ketchup. Honestly, I couldn't eat another bite," Randall returned.

"Ah, c'mon! It's just an itsy-bitsy fly. You've never hurt a fly in your life and couldn't if you tried. So why should it hurt you?" I whined.

Randy stared at the linoleum floor and pondered the thought of eating a bug. He seemed to have gained some confidence in himself, and I could see determination in his eyes. He really, truly wanted to be a Rat.

"OK, but at least let me make a sandwich out of it," Randall chimed, in a sly tone of voice.

"Sure. That's all right," Joe said.

Randy grabbed a piece of bread from Elmo's pantry. Then we proceeded up to his room where Elmo had a live fly contained in a jar. I could tell that Randy wanted to get this over with as quickly as possible. Randy caught the fly and squashed it, stuck it between the bread, and took a whopping bite.

"There!" Randall exclaimed with his mouth full of Wonder Bread. "You goons satisfied? Now what's next?"

"First of all, get yourself and your flybreath out of my room. Fall in, Rats!" Elmo ordered.

Joe led us back to Elmo's kitchen. We were all astonished at how quickly Randy had eaten the fly. It was a record-breaking time and he didn't even wince! We exchanged looks of amazement as we descended the stairs. Joe draped a towel over his arm and used his best French waiter's accent to introduce the next taste adventure.

"After monsieur has had hees ketchup cocktail and hees fly á la sandweech, I am most sure zat he vould like another treat for hees tongue. I now prazent to you, my customaire, our house especiality. Rotten tuna feesh on a stale Vheat Thin! It ess très magnifique!

And I might mention zat it ees our best-selling item. C'est formidable!!" Joe tried furiously to hold in a serious case of the giggles.

He presented Randy with a cracker, on top of which was a generous gob of Elmo's week-old tuna. Randy figured it couldn't be much worse than a fly or ketchup, so he flung the whole thing into his mouth. He attempted a smile, but his mouth could not comply. Randy found himself slugging tap water straight from the faucet to the tune of maniac laughter from our direction.

"Rat Huddle!" I cried. We all bent over in a circle and unanimously voted Randy into our pack.

Joe stood up and cleared his throat. "After much deliberation, the Society of Honorable Rodents has voted you, Mr. Randall P. Snodgrass, an official member of the Rat Pack. I think you will make a fine addition to our club," he stated in a very professional manner.

"Congrats—you're a Rat!" Bobby said as he patted Randall on the back.

"Call 911 and see if you can get my stomach pumped!" Randy gasped.

"Oh, you'll be just fine. True Rats can eat anything and still live," Elmo replied.

"Enough of this initiation junk. Let's go back to the clubhouse and have some real fun," I added.

Randy cried, "Last one there's a rotten Rat!"

In a flash we were off and up to our old mischief, only this time with a new Rat in the pack—another set of sneakers thumpity-thumping, another lifelong friend.

ABOUT THE AUTHOR

Ryan Tate lives in Bellevue, Washington, where he attends Sammamish High School. He wrote this story while attending Odle Middle School, also in Bellevue. Among his interests are basketball, track, piano, and hiking near Mt. Rainier.

Why do *you* sing?

Cricket Song

by CATHERINE PICKUT

An ivory moon hovered unsteadily in the infant twilight as the stars crept nearer to view. Summer bloomed even at night's coming, and the melody of a million crickets filled the air. In a small wooden shanty, a dark-eyed child listened calmly to the falling night.

"Mama?" He only whispered, but she drew close to hear him.

"Yes, child." Her voice carried the warm tones of honey and gentleness that all mothers possess within their souls.

"Why do the crickets sing?"

She looked at her child, brown skin shining softly in the semi-dark. His eyes glistened with the innocent wonder of one who has never tasted pain.

He spoke again, his mouth forming words quickly and carefully. "The birds, they sing 'cause it's they way of bringing joy, and the frogs, they bellow 'cause they happy they frogs instead of polliwogs, but the crickets . . ." His voice faded away.

"Go on, David," she urged him gently.

"The crickets, they don't have any reason. They always been crickets. They not joyful, not glad, they just . . ." He paused, thoughtfully, for a long moment. "They just are."

He rested his head on the sill and watched the sun glimmer away on the hills. The crickets chirped on into the evening mist.

"I don't know, David, I just don't know. But I know that it's nighttime now. And you need your sleep."

The little boy fell into a wondering slumber to the rhapsody of the crickets' song.

David awoke in the hazy dawn, finished his morning chores as quickly as he possibly could, and determined to discover the secret of the crickets' medley once and for all. It was a glorious morning, dew-kissed and sparkling in the rays of a fiery sun. Mr. Laquette's fields of new vegetables reached higher to taste summertime's new warmth and life. And the men toiled there, planting and weeding.

The men were singing quietly into the growing heat.

"Nobody knows the trouble I seen . . ."

David listened to their deep voices carrying the tune. The words were sort of sad, he decided. But the way the strong men sang was almost happy. Somethin' wrong. It seemed broken in its clarity, subdued in its low tones.

David walked up slowly to Jeremiah, a tall bronze man with warm eyes and a muscular build. He tugged at his sleeve gently.

"Well, how're you, Master David? What've you been occupyin' yourself with? Is somethin' on your mind, little man?"

David looked up at the towering man beside him. "Why do you sing when you work?" he asked.

Jeremiah looked at the boy but didn't speak.

So David continued, "The bird sings 'cause he's joyful, and the bullfrog sings 'cause he's happy bein' a frog, but why do you sing?"

Jeremiah got a kind of pondering look on his face. "I guess we sing because it makes things go faster—the work, I mean. Why you wonder?"

David shrugged. Jeremiah went back to his work.

David squinted at the sun. The temperature increased quickly in the fields of summer. To make the work go faster? No, that was not why the crickets sang. The crickets sounded different from the men in the field, but David wasn't sure why. The crickets' song was perfect and pure, and so different. Something not there in the men's dark voices.

He went to find his mother. She worked in the big house, in the kitchen. It smelled of prosperity in the big house, of silk and cotton. But the air also smelled of baked beans, his mother's baked beans.

The big house stood, white and clean, at the front of the plantation. David didn't go in very often, and always through the back door. But he could hear his mother's silken voice humming a soft tune as he stood at the door.

"Mama?"

"David, did you finish your work? Did you remember to take care of the goats?"

Yes, David had done all of that earlier, during the

cooler hours.

"Yes, Mama."

"So what's troublin' you?"

David thought for a moment.

"Mama, why you hummin' when you work?"

Mama looked at her child. "I don't know. I like the tune, I suppose. No reason, really." She turned back to the breakfast dishes. "Run along now. Master won't like you hangin' on his back door all day." She smiled.

David walked away, kicking a round stone. Mama sang just for singin'. Jeremiah sang 'cause it made his work go faster. But their songs were different from the crickets'. He liked the crickets' song. It made him feel a dull pulse of peace way down deep inside of him. Mama's song was just a song, and Jeremiah's was kind of sad. But not like the cricket. Somethin' missin' in Mama's song, somethin' more missin' in Jeremiah's. But what?

David scurried to do his afternoon work. By evening, his eleven-year-old body tingled from effort. He sat in silence by the window and felt the crickets' song grow in intensity. It was more wonderful now, and he could tell the difference had become clearer and more dis- tinct, though he couldn't feel quite what. But it was still there.

"Looks like good weather tomorrow, doesn't it, child?" Mama knew that the blood-red sky meant a glorious day tomorrow. The shades of crimson and fire exploded on the horizon as the sun sank quickly into the earth. They sat in silence, letting the song of the tawny gold meadow fall into syncopation with the crickets' cries of life.

Finally, it was lavender darkness enfolding mother

and son. The crickets' chorus grew deafening in the moon's glow.

"Mama?"

"Yes, child."

"The bird sings 'cause he's joyful, the bullfrog croaks 'cause he's happy he's a frog, Jeremiah sings 'cause it makes his work easier, and you sing 'cause you want to . . ."

His dark eyes surveyed the meadow one more time before he continued. "And I know why the cricket sings, Mama. And why it sounds so sweet."

The woman closed her eyes for a moment. "Why's that, David?"

Some time passed, one of those times that seems an eternity but is only an eye's blink in truth. A breeze tickled the tops of the meadow wheat. David stood and took a long, deep breath of sweet summer air. A dying star tore a seam in the sky as he opened his mouth to speak. He looked at his mother.

"The cricket sings . . ."

He glanced up at the pearly moon again. It sparkled like a shiny nickel at the bottom of a wishing well. The crickets kept chirruping, their song rising to charm the stars into twinkling. David sighed and looked out over the field before he finished.

"The cricket sings . . . 'cause he's free. Just 'cause he's free."

His mother rose and stood by him as the sun's last warm glow faded away. Together, they watched night cover heaven's face and listened to the song washing across the meadow. They listened, in wonder, to the song which they could never sing.

ABOUT THE AUTHOR

Catherine Pickut lives in Wellsville, New York, where she attends Wellsville High School. She wrote and submitted her story while attending Wellsville Middle School. Among her interests are the cello, piano, and debating.

To save her people, Kanya
would have to master her fear.

Beneath a Dark Mountain

by Jessica Hekman

PREFACE

In the universe there are an infinite number of worlds
and their suns. In one space of Infinity, circling twin
suns, whirls a planet that embodies all the dreams
of Earth. Across this planet's face roam unicorns, drag-
ons, and elves. Living near a mountain range in the
North are a few humans and rukhs.*

Five decades before this tale, a small tribe of humans called the Alitarril fled the attack of the Onyarx,
a dark race of nightmares almost human in appear-
ance, but short and round, with snubbed pig's noses
and little black pig's eyes. The humans were driven up
into the mountains and beyond, down to the valley
below, where they were trapped. At the far side of this
valley roared a ceaseless fire.

For a while, doom seemed certain, but when the

---

*Rukhs (pronounced "rocks") are a legendary race of giant birds and
are commonly referred to as rocs. [author's note]

Alitarril entered the valley, they had woken the rukhs of the mountains. As the Onyarx passed the rukhs in pursuit of the humans, some regrettable incident occurred; perhaps some rukh was killed. The two races set upon each other, with the Alitarril waiting for fifty years as the war raged on, knowing all the while that whoever won it would come and kill them. And all the while they cursed their forefathers.

But the rukhs were not content with battling their lives away. And a cold winter came, forcing the humans to seek fire . . .

The fire grew hotter on Kanya's cheeks as she jogged along, her red braid swinging with uncharacteristic heaviness behind her. She stopped for a moment and set down the smoothly oiled stick, leaning it carefully against a rock, to tug at the offending braid. She hated having her hair up, but her mentor, Arlla, had said she must—to make her way through the Briars . . .

Well, the Briars are long past, thought Kanya defiantly, starting to untwine her hair. She felt guilty as the first strands fell across her cheeks, then frightened as she thought of the Never-Ending Fire, and bound it up again hastily. She picked up the torch and ran her fingers over its smooth surface, feeling the lovingly polished and oiled wood.

I will be sorry when this torch burns, Kanya thought grimly. She closed her eyes and thought of the red glow in the sky becoming more brilliantly malevolent by the night, until it was faintly visible even in the day. Kanya opened her eyes and stuck the torch in her belt. She would do this for her people. They needed the fire because it would be a cold winter in the valley, and none would survive without heat. Fire was the alternative to crossing the mountains en route to warmer lands . . .

Curse the Fathers! thought Kanya as she jogged on again. *Had they no more sense than to be driven through the mountains where the rukhs dwell, and to the very edge of the fire-lands? Were the Onyarx more clever, then, to have outmaneuvered the Fathers?*

Kanya's breath began to come in hot, painful gasps. Her lungs hurt. Still, she smiled to herself at the amusing thought. *An Onyar clever? Never!* She had seen one once as it scouted through the valley. Her father and brother had killed it. Her eyes closed at the bloody memory.

The heat grew so intense that at last Kanya looked up. Just ahead on the horizon was the fire. Its lashing flames snarled and leaped into the air, only to fall back hissing at the barrier of trenches built by the Ancients, who had lived in the valley before the coming of the Alitarril. The scalding wind whipped at Kanya and she stopped. She was quite close enough now! She stared at the fire resentfully. Why must it be beautiful? It was deadly and evil. But the red-gold of its flames hummed at her, the Fire-Haired One, she who was said to be the child of fire herself.

Kanya jerked her gaze away. The fire was far too hot for her to get any closer. Not thirty yards away, already it dominated her vision and caused lights to dance in her head when she closed her eyes. This was the part of her journey that she had dreaded. How could she get any fire now? Her people needed fire to live—winter was coming, and with the autumn wind's harsh portent, they knew it would be a bad winter. If the Alitarril had no fire, how would they live?

It's not my fault! Kanya screamed silently. *I was born to this! Why must I get us out? . . . I didn't have to. It was just that we need fire. Arlla thought I should go. It wasn't a vote or anything; she just said I should go, and it seemed like a good idea at the time, so I went. Why didn't I ask someone to come? Why didn't I even tell anyone I was going? I know Arlla influenced my decision; she does that. They say that when she lost the use of her legs she gained greater use of her brain. It's true that she all but rules the village. They also say that, outside of the valley, you needn't grow up so fast. I'm only sixteen . . .*

Kanya sat down with the unlit torch beside her and sighed. If she couldn't get any closer to the fire, how could she get the torch lit so that her people would be warm this winter?

The wind engulfed her, howling like an animal. *Is this how a rukh calls?* she wondered. *I've never seen a rukh. Arlla has . . . that's how she was crippled, they say. I've heard that the rukh broke both her legs, and the tigre Sinnla found her and dragged her back . . . but not in time; she's crippled now and can't walk.*

Kanya thought of Sabre, her own white tigre. The tigres were staunch friends of the Alitarril, unlike the rukhs, who lived in the upper reaches of the mountains above the Onyarx. Rukhs were unpredictable, and surely warlike to have fought the Onyarx for fifty years. Kanya closed her eyes again, then opened them and whispered: "May I never see a rukh in my lifetime!" The slowly spoken words died on the whistling wind.

The wind howled again, and a glowing spark flew toward Kanya. *What luck!* she thought, running forward. The spark caught a bush and blazed up. It was, in an instant, too hot to approach. Kanya bit her lip and edged closer. The heat flamed on her bare face and she closed her eyes, shielding them behind an upflung arm. Kanya grimaced and thought, *I have to do this*. But the fire was laughing at her, and she was still so far away!

She crept closer, intent on the nearest spark. The world began to swim with the omnipotent heat, and, staggering backward, she finally thought, *It's not worth it*. She thought about giving up just as a shadow crossed the sky.

Allin circled lower, watching the girl with the long, loose braid that was so red as to be nearly vermilion. *She'll never make it,* he thought, wondering why she seemed so intent on getting herself scorched. He'd seen her fight her way through the thick brambles commonly called the Briars, and had considered offering her a ride back. She was very small, and he liked her spirit. Allin glided lower still as the breeze carrying him died. He watched intently as the girl again crept closer—closer—*why didn't she give up?* With a sudden small sigh, barely audible even to Allin's sharp ears, she sank to the ground.

The rukh swooped down next to her, thinking, *Well, she's done it now.* He beat his wings gently, fanning the fire back, managed to take off again, and, as he hovered above her, picked her up in his talons. It seemed to him that she was very light, barely heavier than one of his own feathers. He glided up higher.

"Let's see," Allin murmured in his strange, grating

language. "She comes from that little village to the north . . ."

Kanya shifted, then abruptly awoke and sat up. Her older sister, Anya, was watching her closely.

Kanya batted Anya's hand away from her forehead. "I'm fine and I *don't* have a fever. Let me be! How'd I get back here?"

"Allin. He's the rukh that brought you back not even an hour ago. He set you down in the middle of the village and has been trying to make us trust him ever since. We've decided that he's trustworthy." Anya hesitated; it seemed that the rukh was still not *absolutely* trusted.

"*A rukh?* Rukhs are enemies!"

Anya shrugged. "Not Allin, it seems. Well, I guess you can get up now if you want to see him."

Kanya promptly got out of bed and pulled on some clothes with childish impatience.

"Kanya?" The voice was very deep and heavily accented, barely recognizable. "Anya, is she conscious? Send her out." The rukh's voice was harsh and forced, as though he were spitting out the unfamiliar words. He stressed the first syllable of every word, whether it ought to have been stressed or not. This was a habit that Kanya soon found irritating.

Kanya tied a band around her head to keep her long, loose hair out of her eyes and stalked out, furious with this Allin rukh for calling her out. But when she saw him, she froze. He was gigantic! Looking down at her from a considerable distance, he appeared at least forty feet tall. Kanya regarded him with a touch more respect.

"I want to talk to you," said Allin. "I've spoken to your village already."

Kanya looked around desperately, feeling cornered. Arlla was slumped in her chair, near Allin, grinning at Kanya from ear to ear. Sinnla and Sabre were beside her. She trotted over to stand between the two tigres and nodded at Allin, her hand resting lightly on Sabre's head.

"We rukhs have been your friends," began Allin thickly. "But as you have feared us, we too have feared you. I have spoken to my people on behalf of the Al—Altari—on behalf of your village, and the rukhs agreed that if I spoke with you they might . . . help.

"We fight a common enemy. With fire, we can trap the Onyarx, then cross the fire—your people on the backs of my people—to safety. Come with me. You seem to know the dangers of the fire; you have experience."

Kanya watched the rukh carefully, especially his fiery black eyes. At last she nodded. "I will help you because my kinspeople have consented. But I don't understand."

The rukh nodded briefly. "Do you know that the Onyarx are as afraid of fire as your people? They live far from it, and when they burn campfires, they are always carefully controlled. If we place a raging fire at Darrs's two exits, they will be trapped."

Kanya frowned. "It's a mountain. Exits?"

"A very steep mountain. There are only two slender passes which slope gently enough to allow exit. I will take you now. Your fallen torch awaits you by the fire," said the rukh. He looked down at Kanya. "Is there anything you want to bring?"

"Yes. A cloak." Anya materialized behind her sister with a long gray one, and Kanya pulled it over her shoulders and fastened it securely.

"I think the comfortable place for you to ride would be on my back," the rukh continued, "but my feathers are very smooth and you might slip. It would be best if I carried you as I did when I returned you home."

"Excuse me?" muttered Kanya, watching suspiciously as the huge bird lifted its wings. He walked awkwardly away, until he was a little way beyond the village center. Kanya scrambled to follow him.

Allin brought his wings down so forcefully that the wind they generated knocked Kanya flat. Then Allin was in the air, hovering, extending his talons.

"Grab on!" he commanded. Kanya flung an arm over one hooked nail and was promptly lifted up.

As they rose higher into the air, Kanya gritted her teeth and did not look down. Allin curved his talons into a hard seat where Kanya wriggled around in a vain attempt to get comfortable.

"Don't slip out!" the rukh called, hoarsely casting the foreign words to a whipping wind. His voice sounded very high up and far away.

The Briars, nearly a quarter of a mile of thick brambles, passed quickly beneath them. Kanya watched in fascination, remembering the problem they had been for her! Then the fire came into view. It was licking very near the fallen torch already. Kanya frowned.

"It was not that near when I dropped the torch."

"The fire's been growing," replied Allin, rolling his r's slightly. His voice was still thick, but shriller when struck by the heavy wind. "It's this wind," he explained.

"It's pushing the fire closer to the Alitarril. Soon your people will be driven up into the mountains and . . ."

And the Onyarx, thought Kanya sadly. "How am I ever going to get the thing, then?" she yelled into the wind.

"What? The torch? You'll see."

Allin landed a bit nearer to the fire than was comfortable, and Kanya slipped out of his talons to hide behind a leg. "Ow! It's hot!" she complained.

Allin shrugged her off and raised his wings. Kanya flung one arm around his leg and another over her eyes to protect against the heat. His wings began to descend, slowly, then faster, until Kanya could hear the wind whistling around them. She bit her lip in anticipation of being knocked flat again and grabbed Allin's leg more tightly with both arms.

The fire shifted in the resulting wind, while Kanya, sheltered by Allin's leg, managed miraculously to stay up. "Now!" Allin shouted, "while the fire's driven back!"

Kanya ran forward. The heat reflected off her cloak, but she could feel her unprotected cheeks growing red. Grimly, she pressed forward.

Kanya heard a faint whooshing sound, which grew louder, and then the wind from Allin's wings knocked her flat again! "Darn," she groaned, face in the dirt. She looked back over her shoulder at Allin with a black glare.

"Run! Hurry!"

Suddenly she realized that she had to get that torch *now!* She charged forward, barely on her feet, and grabbed it. It was blazing hot and burning at one end. She wrapped a corner of her cloak around it and held that. The fire came rushing back, straight at her. She stumbled back, biting her lip. If Allin chose to blow on the fire now, she'd be knocked into it . . .

The heat was infernal. Kanya regained her balance, turned, and ran. Allin's wing twitched and the fire wavered slightly in the wind. She drew closer to the tall bird and, simultaneously, felt the fire drawing nearer to her.

Allin thrust his beak toward her, his eyes urgent. She grabbed it and scrambled up. His head lifted as he took off.

As soon as the bumpy takeoff was over, Kanya slid forward into a position similar to riding a tigre. "Don't speak!" she warned Allin, "or you'll knock me right off!" She patted his beak with a grin. "Thanks," she smiled.

Allin rumbled deep in his chest at the familiarity, but flew on.

They flew right past the village of the Alitarril. Kanya looked back sharply at Allin's eyes. *Can't you see because I'm in the way?* she thought. *There's my village!* But she did not want him to answer her question and knock her off his beak—it was a long way to the ground.

They kept going, straight on, until the mountains loomed ahead. Allin banked and finally landed at the base of a mountain. He lowered his bill to the ground, and Kanya slipped off, glaring at him.

"What are you doing?" she snapped. "There are Onyarx up there. They'll kill me!"

Allin regarded her silently for a moment before speaking. "They might kill me as well. I think that my death is rather more probable—don't you? You can hide." His voice held no malice, only stark fact.

Kanya looked at those fiery black eyes and thought,

He's really going to kill himself for his people! And my people! I should be willing to die, too. But I'm not!

"Why are we here?" she asked him curtly, holding the fiery torch low so that the glare wouldn't obstruct her line of vision.

He whispered—and it is interesting to hear a rukh whisper—"We are going to set fire to the base of Darrs Mountain, and to the world of the Onyarx within it."

His whispering caressed Kanya like a breeze, and when he said "fire," he rolled his *r* as a true rukh should. She shivered as he misused one word—"world" instead of "settlement"; it made him seem alien, not the Allin she had known for—how long? Only a few hours, but it seemed a year. He looked nervous: every so often he shifted from foot to foot, as Kanya had seen sparrows do. She had never heard him stumble when speaking her language, but when she saw the black pools of flame that should have been eyes, she said nothing and waited.

"The Onyarx will be trapped as they ought—as they have trapped us and you."

"*You* are trapped?" Kanya looked up at the towering rukh, thought of the man-sized Onyar she'd seen killed, and thought again: *Trapped?*

"The Onyarx do know some little magic," replied the rukh quietly. "All black. We cannot cross the mountains or the fire. It is a form of—how do you say it? They hold a curse over us: this is the only mountain that will ever be our home, and if we go to another, our eggs will have thin shells and will break when we warm them; food will be scarce and we will grow sick . . ." He glanced away from her, up at his home. "Fire," he added, "it is cleansing. It will destroy the spell. We will escape."

Kanya lifted her torch and said, "We will live, my friend, to take them away from here ourselves."

Allin watched her torch burning low and red, then nodded. He lifted his wings once again beneath the glowing sky, the stars brilliant against the blanket of blackness. He said, "I am accustomed to flying from the heights of cliffs. This is the last time I'll take off from the ground today."

Kanya grabbed his talons and slipped eel-like into them as the rukh lifted her from the ground. They flapped higher, his wings straining, and the mountains were thrown into such stark relief that Kanya shivered again. She was not cold. "I never knew—they look so peaceful from the village."

A few small, carefully contained Onyarx fires glowed in pinpoints on the hillsides. The jagged cliffs reared up sharply, cut and scarred vilely by the roads of the Onyarx. A dark, heavy, putrid smell drifted steadily up, marking the presence of Onyarx. A few caves gutted the hills, empty and lean. Hunger and fear were in the air.

The rukh glided slowly—silently—higher, until the air grew thin and Kanya nearly choked. Then he swerved sharply to one side and landed in a mountain nest.

"Illai?" he called softly. He curled up one leg to safely hide Kanya. A smaller, lighter colored rukh edged out of the shadows.

"Time?" he rasped, his Alitarril barely recognizable.

"It is." In a barely audible voice Allin said, "This is Illai. He will take you to the base of the mountains to set your fire, while I speak to the other rukhs. They will be ready when you return."

Kanya twisted around and stared up at him: *Must I go with a strange rukh?*

"Illai is to be trusted. He is smaller and lighter than I, and not as opinionated as some. I am the only one who can sway the other rukhs; I did do one small thing for them that will be remembered, I think. Now go. I do not trust the Onyarx; they are cunning and therefore good at hiding about our aeries at night."

Kanya was gently transferred to Illai, who glided off the mountain. Kanya tried to burn neither him nor herself with her torch and thought, *I never knew Allin was so big until I saw Illai! These talons are small!*

They crossed the mountains at a high speed, Illai straining to fly as fast as he could. "There, little one," he told her in an accent so thick as to be barely understandable. "Set red heat about these!"

The bushes were parched from lack of water and had never seen fire in their lives. Kanya struck about her with the torch so that hot flames sprang up. Illai fanned them gently back, in a circle around the base of the mountain. Kanya ran ever faster, her feet aching, trying to beat time—she must hurry before she was discovered.

Illai was always behind her, wings fanning gently, carefully forcing the fire to stay where they wanted it, his bill gouging trenches to guide the fire in a close circle around the small mountain's base. Soon the rukh began to pull up bracken and set it in bare places, so that the fire caught at it and roared hungrily, blazing up.

"Good," he said at last, taking her cloak abruptly in his beak and lifting her up into the air. Kanya, gasping for breath, reached up and hung on to his beak. They flew only about a quarter of a mile before Illai said, placing her gently on the ground, "More red heat must set here. Heat on both sides—surround!"

Kanya ran, pressing the torch deep into the dry branches. Her hands were scraped from twigs and thorns, and her arms ached. Faster! She must keep on outrunning the hungry fire . . .

"Enough. Will burn on its own," said Illai, at last. "Go back."

Gratefully, Kanya grabbed the bill he offered her. He lifted her up over his shoulder and set her gently down on his back.

"Easy now . . . feathers slippery."

"Slippery and big as mallee leaves," muttered Kanya, thinking of the six-foot leaves of a particular tree. Illai chuckled, beating his way laboriously up into the air.

The pointed cliff rose up in front of them. As soon as they landed, Kanya tumbled off Illai and ran to Allin. He was speaking earnestly with a big bird in his own language, but turned at Kanya's shout. Lowering his beak, he said, "Hush, little one. You are back sound?"

Safe and sound, Kanya thought, but she only nodded and touched his beak in greeting. Allin tried to return her smile—or so it seemed—but his beak could not twist up into a grin like hers, and he shrugged.

"This is Miunatin," he announced, "the Mother. Our leader. I saved her life from an Onyar when her wing was wounded—thus I do have some little influence over our people. They will come. And the fire—?" He broke off, looking back at the base of the mountain. Already smoke was rising.

"Good, little one. Now, Illai, you may come; we

go to set a fire to the settlement at Darrs Mountain."

Kanya raised her torch. It was burning low. "We must hurry."

The other rukhs watched as the trio glided gently off the mountain. Kanya swallowed convulsively as they drifted lower, nearer to the Onyarx, bane of the Alitarril, at Darrs . . .

They landed on a ledge a little beyond the fort. Kanya's eyes instantly focused on the huge iron gates and the scattered huts within. A few Onyarx guards stood, only half-vigilant, at Darrs's entrance. Kanya could see that the village was fairly open, but deeply shadowed. And the huts would burn nicely.

"Go quickly," hissed Allin. "I'll distract them." Kanya slipped off (her heart was in her mouth, so she swallowed it) and ran, unobserved, toward Darrs's gates.

Allin jumped off the ledge with a shriek and a howl, bringing Darrs's Onyarx running. He made a great commotion on the ground, flapping his wing as if it were wounded.

"Hurry!" called Illai, as Kanya charged past the distracted guards and through the gates. He motioned to the spears and arrows that the Onyarx were gathering. "Death," said the young rukh.

Not Allin—he could never die, thought Kanya.

It was very dark, and she ran in the shadows and with the shadows. The stink of the piggish Onyarx filled her nose and stomach; she gagged. They were all over, like maggots. Kanya remembered—just in time—to shield the torch's glow with her body. Perhaps, hunkered over like this, she would appear to be an Onyar—at least, to the bleary eyes of an Onyar. *Quickly now, before they see the gleam of the torch!*

Kanya began setting the fire, praying that the torch would last just a moment longer. Soon the blaze was crackling wildly, and Onyarx were running toward her.

Abandoning the torch to the fire, Kanya ran an obstacle course around the clumsy creatures. Ahead were the gates! Allin, beyond, raised his head in surprise when he saw her; Illai started forward but was too far away. She was almost to the gates when panic set in and the world began to spin. She stumbled . . .

A heavy hand clamped down on her shoulder and whipped her around. She stared into the leering face of an Onyar.

Meanwhile, Allin's "wounded" wing had become a sweeping arc, knocking down Onyarx in a huge semicircle around him. He had long since given up the game of being wounded and was fighting for his life. Two arrows, mere pins to him, were embedded in his wings. He saw the Onyar draw his knife, ready for a quick kill, and tried to run to Kanya's aid. But the rukh's talons were not made for running, and he had to hop awkwardly, calling Illai to help him.

Luckily the Onyar did not seem inclined toward a quick kill, and he was too absorbed in Kanya to notice the quiet rukh or the horrified screams of his people. As the knife cut her arm, Illai's beak descended and swung sideways, knocking the Onyar away.

The creature was flung fifteen feet and landed hard, but he was tough as iron and sat up only a little dizzily. When he saw Kanya getting away, he grabbed a spear, drew it back, and aimed carefully for a one-chance throw.

Allin beat his wings, trying unsuccessfully to take

off. Wings half-extended, he hopped forward for a running start, Kanya hanging on to one thick leg.

Suddenly there was a *thunk* above her. Kanya looked up to see Allin's belly shudder, then right itself.

"I'm fine," the rukh called. "But you may have to ride Illai out . . ." His voice was faint.

Kanya closed her eyes against the hard world and the heat as Allin finally got beyond the gates. With one last surge of rukhian strength, he fairly tossed her to Illai, and in an instant Kanya and Illai were in the air. Kanya peeked out from her cradle in Illai's legs and looked down at Allin, who was still trying to take off.

The big rukh was flapping his wings desperately, hordes of Onyarx closing in. Only now could Kanya see the hindering spear embedded to its butt in his wing. She drew in her breath as another spear sank into his belly. Now the Onyarx were circling him, throwing spear after spear. At last the great rukh turned away and sank down near the fire. He never twitched.

"Illai!" screamed Kanya. "They're killing him! Go back! Save him!"

"Is already dead," replied Illai.

"But he was my *friend!*" cried Kanya.

"Was my father," snapped Illai, his words very guttural and forced.

Kanya had thought that Allin would never die. Now he was dead. He would never see the freedom he had given his life for. Kanya curled up and sobbed.

The Alitarril and the rukhs gathered swiftly and quietly in the dark, hardly speaking. Kanya sat outside her house with her friend Sabre pressed up against her in feline silence. Sabre fended off all the Alitarril who wished to thank Kanya, keeping her alone as she wished to be.

Illai whispered something to Miunatin, and she nodded. "It is time to fly," Illai announced, "over the fire to a new land."

The Alitarril were already climbing awkwardly onto some birds, lugging their belongings up behind them. Kanya stared up at Illai. "Can't I just stay?" she asked.

"Our people are alike. Feel much the same," replied Illai. "But life worth living, will find, little one. I take comfort in that have you."

His eyes, very cautious now, were hard and dark as he said this, the light fire of life gone; it was a chance he was taking. Kanya looked up into those black jewels—how unlike Allin's fiery eyes!—and nodded her tear-streaked face. Illai lowered his beak and carefully picked up Sabre, to set him on his dark back. Then he offered his bill to Kanya.

Kanya bit her lip and allowed herself to be raised up.

"Now we go!" called Illai, and the rukhs and Alitarril all flew up high over the fire, into the rosy sunrise.

ABOUT THE AUTHOR

Jessica Hekman lives in Claremont, California, where she attends Vivian Webb School. "Beneath a Dark Mountain," mostly written when she attended Pioneer Jr. High School, in Upland, won recognition in the Promising Young Writers Program sponsored by the National Council of Teachers of English.

The search continues for Ms. Right . . .

A Day at the Mall

by MARK HARRIS

From the soles of her Nike Cross Trainers to the top of her long brown hair, she was an all-around babe.

I turned to my left. "Not bad, huh?"

Tom started to laugh. "Like you'd have a chance—right!"

"Darn right I would."

Tom and I were pretty good friends, and, for some reason, insulting each other was part of our relationship.

As the girl I was rudely staring at passed, I heard her talking with her friend and found out that her name was Jen.

There were a lot of girls at the Burlington Mall, but Jen was definitely the best. Tom and I left our posts near The Sharper Image and began to follow my future wife and her friend. The two girls turned their heads and saw us following them.

This is where the chase begins, I thought to myself.

They took sharp turns around corners, ducked into large crowds, and then, knowing that we would never follow them in, walked into a lingerie shop to catch their breath and plan their next route.

A few minutes later, the two girls left the store and we began to follow them again. Suddenly they stopped and turned around. I was across from Jen. She was even better looking at this distance, a mere five feet! Everything was perfect. Now all I had to do was wait for them to say something, then respond by asking Jen if she wanted to go to the movies.

"Hi," Jen's friend said in a high-pitched voice.

"Hi," Tom blurted out before I could.

"My name is Kim and this is Jen."

Jen brushed up her bangs and tossed her hair over her right shoulder.

Then our eyes met. It was destiny. I could see it now—two kids, big house, a Beamer, a cocker spaniel . . .

"Hey, Jen, do you want to go see a movie?"

. . . a tennis court, pool . . . Hold on. Tom just asked out Jen!

The girls turned to each other and giggled for a minute. In the meantime I had slapped Tom across the top of his head twice. She was going to be the mother of my children, not Tom's girlfriend! I couldn't believe that he asked her out. I mean, we all knew what she was going to say, but that wasn't the point.

"What the heck's wrong with you? I was going to ask her out. You wouldn't have even seen her if it wasn't for me," I whispered to him.

"Sure, I'd love to," Jen said.

I had heard of playing hard to get, but really! I didn't know what to do, but as the couple stared at me, I sort of got the hint.

I turned to Kim. "Well, ahhh . . ." I wanted to know how long it took her to perfect that hairdo with the "wave" in the front. And where in the world did she get those large, flashy, cheap earrings? "Ummm, do you want to go with them?"

"Yeah, why not?"

So we started walking to the movie theater. I wanted to just run over to Jen, take her by the elbow, spin her toward me, and . . .

"You're really cute," Jen whispered to Tom.

. . . and ask her what her favorite song was.

I was still extremely mad at Tom for stealing my girl, a girl who was wearing tight jeans and had a really nice Levi's patch on her back pocket. She also had on a loose sweater with a V-shaped collar. Her hair was that perfect long brown stuff, right out of the shampoo commercials.

"She likes Tom, you know," Kim interrupted.

"Excuse me?"

"I said that Jen likes Tom."

"That's nice." My life picture was fading.

We finally got to the movies and bought tickets to *The Hunt for Red October*. Tom paid for Jen and that may have been why Kim got mad when I didn't pay for her. We found some good seats, four in a row. During the previews I told Kim that I had to go to the bathroom.

"Hi, Mom." (God, this was low.) "Can you pick us up now?"

"Yeah. Is something wrong?"

"No, we're just bored."

"OK."

I went back to my seat just as the movie was beginning. After the credits, a submarine surfaced through crashing waves. I looked at Kim's hair, you know, just to check "the wave." She turned her head and gave me "the look." Time to finish Jen and Tom's relationship, because, if I couldn't have her, no one would.

"Tom, we gotta go. It's three o'clock."

"We're not getting picked up until five."

"We're getting picked up now. Come on," I lied. It was about to work out perfectly, and Tom would never see Jen again. But I would see her next weekend at the mall. "Let's go! My mom's gonna kill me if we're late."

"Are you serious?"

"Yes. Hurry up." Then Tom destroyed my little plan.

"Hey, Jen, what's your phone number?" He scratched it into his dry skin.

Kim asked me if I wanted her phone number, but I told her that my skin was really moist. Tom and I ran through the mall to meet my mom at the other end. Sure enough, she was there. And it was raining out—hope Tom doesn't forget about the number! But he did, and it went away when his arm got wet.

I never did see Jen again, but I will always remember her.

ABOUT THE AUTHOR

Mark Harris lives in Weston, Massachusetts, where he attends Weston High School. He wrote this story while at Weston Middle School. He reports: "During my spare time I like to listen to the radio, play a lot of tennis, and go to the mall and movies with friends."

"If I had said those three words,
would his life have been any happier?"

My Father

by SARAH ORVIS

The afternoon sun shone brightly on the white sands of the beach, and I turned my eyes away, something I had been doing very often lately.

From farther down along the shore, the happy squeals of a child caught my ears. A father and his young son chased each other over the small dunes, the father walking only slightly fast so the child could outrun him. He caught his son and lifted him way up high, twirling him around before placing him on his shoulders and heading back to the parking lot.

My father died a month ago. He'd been as healthy as anyone could expect a 38-year-old man to be. He'd gone to sleep one night and just never got up in the morning. The doctor told us it was internal bleeding caused by a ruptured kidney. Nothing could've been done to help him, he said. I thought otherwise.

I picked up a small shell and threw it, watching as it floated for a moment before a wave drowned it.

I was my father's only son, the eldest of three kids. Stacy and Jen, my little sisters, were only one and three, and would never know their father, never recall his loud, booming laugh or, less regrettably, the sting of his hand on their backsides.

I suppose I could say that he was a good father, better than most I know, anyway. He always had a ready smile, a kind word, and advice that could turn even the worst of times around. When I was little, he'd take me fishing, or to the park, and all the places you go to as a child. We were close then, and I couldn't have looked up to anyone more. I wanted to grow up to be just like Dad.

Then things began to change. I became too old to go fishing, could never find time to do stuff with him anymore, though I know I could have made time. I remember days when I caught a wistful, almost sad look from him aimed at me, especially on winter mornings perfect for snowmen and snowballs.

There were times when we fought, and, although I can't remember what we fought about, I know it was I who usually started it. He was a man of quiet simplicity, and I was a boy with a head crammed with all the things that go through the minds of young children. He was stuck in old ways, and nothing he hadn't seen was real in his eyes. I readily accepted anything new that came my way.

Dad tried to talk to me, but it was hard on both of us. He had become shameful in my eyes then. You see, my father had never learned to read, and he'd dropped out of high school as soon as he could to take a job in an auto repair shop. Later, he saved enough money to start his own. We were not rich, but we were far from poor. This should have satisfied me, but I was still ashamed of my father. The terrible thing is—I think he knew it.

Then he started to behave oddly. He'd stay up late into the night, and in the morning would appear in the kitchen like a zombie, dark circles under his eyes. But those eyes had taken on a gleam, and he often shot glances at me that were full of something I tried to name, but could not. Not until one night.

It was winter, and I woke when a branch fell outside. The wind roared, and the cold had worked its way through the walls and into my bed, so I decided to get another blanket from the hall closet.

The kitchen light was still on, and I walked through the living room to shut it off. Peering around the corner, I saw my father at the kitchen table, with a book in front of him and a pen in his hand. His head was nodding, but he shook himself awake to take a gulp of what, I am sure, was cold coffee. As I watched, he began talking slowly and quietly. After a time I could catch snippets of what he was saying and recognized Dr. Seuss's *Cat in the Hat*.

I had bought that book years ago when I was little, after saving up my allowance. I'd brought it home and given it to my father, asking him to read it to me. I remember his face, how red it was, and how sorry his eyes were as he handed it back to me. All he said was, "Sorry, Son." I remember feeling confused. I left the book on the kitchen counter and when I looked for it again, it was gone. I hadn't seen it since. But now I heard the familiar rhymes coming from my father's lips. I was stunned.

He was teaching himself to read, struggling with

each word. Yet even that amazed me.

I stood in that corner for a long time. My father knew I was there, I'm sure, because I was none too quiet coming down those stairs. I think he wanted me to know.

I went back to bed without the extra blanket. The warmth in my heart was all I needed.

I never mentioned my discovery. But my faith and respect for my father grew stronger, and time and again I found myself turning to him for advice. I spent time with him each day, and we grew close again, talking about everything and nothing at all.

Jen was born, and I took time off from school to work side by side with Dad at the shop to pay the bills. I wasn't very good at mechanics, but Dad was patient and took the time to teach me. Even though he owned the place, he preferred being under a car, covered with grease, to sitting in an office, sorting bills and receipts.

We went to baseball games together, he came to my football tournaments, and I rediscovered my love of fishing. He was there when I graduated from school, and I was there when he received his high school diploma, twenty years after he'd dropped out. The mysterious gleam I had seen in his eyes now had a name. It was pride.

Stacy was born, and we tumbled into hard times again. I took a night job at a movie theatre and worked with Dad during the day. I put my dreams of college on hold and became his full-time partner.

One summer day, just two months before his death, I came home to find a gray Pontiac in our yard, parked where my hand-me-down Chevy usually was. My father was sitting casually on the hood, and as I began to question, he silenced me. I deserved it, he said. I had worked hard, and I needed a car that started when I wanted it to, unlike my Chevy.

We didn't have money to spare, I knew. Yet he cared enough to take the risk. The three words I had not uttered in fifteen years were now on the tip of my tongue, but still I could not tell him that I loved him. I knew it showed in my eyes, though, because I could see the reflection of it in his, which were as wet and shiny as mine. We didn't need those words.

At his funeral, we made a very small procession: my mother and sisters, a few close relatives, some guys from the garage, and me. My mother was a pallid stone throughout the ceremony, and Jen fell asleep. I didn't cry, although the tears were there. Later I cried for hours, alone.

As I stood on the beach where we once played, a heavy sadness hung in my heart, and I knew it would never quite go away. We'd been through a lot, he and I, and all I could hope for now was that I could somehow find the strength to carry on without him. I wondered, if I had said those three words, would his life have been any happier? Maybe. But I hadn't needed to say it. He'd known anyway.

I walked back to the parking lot, where my gray Pontiac awaited me. It started right up.

About the Author

Sarah Orvis lives in Bristol, New Hampshire, where she attends Newfound Memorial Middle School. Her hobbies include biking, swimming, volleyball, track, drawing, reading, and, "of course, writing." Sarah also plays many musical instruments, her favorite being the flute.

God vs. Goddess: It was the trial of eternity.

In Defense of Hades

by SARAH-SCOTT BRETT

Your Honor, ladies and gentlemen of the jury, honored guests, the plaintiff would lead you to believe that my client, Hades, is a cruel, evil god, who stole a young woman from her innocent existence and caused much trauma. Such is the nasty, untruthful picture painted by the overprotective mother of a bored young goddess. From extensive research, thorough investigation, and in-depth interviews with innumerable gods, humans, and other assorted beings, I have discovered the truth.

Let me begin at the beginning. After the Titanic Wars, led by Zeus and his two brothers, there was much organizing to do. The brothers (Zeus, Poseidon, and Hades) decided to draw lots to decide who got what realm. You see, ladies and gentlemen, none of them wanted the underworld! None of them. So, when it was over and Hades was stuck with it, there was no possibility of compromise. As a matter of fact, Hades begged, literally begged Zeus to allow him to change to a nomadic reign, one that would allow him to roam and be the god of travelers, and to give the underworld to one of his yet-to-be-born sons. But Zeus, the ruler of all, decided that he would rather exile his brother than one of his own sons.

Now, I want to stop here a minute to make an important point: Up until that time, Hades was a young, kind god who loved the sun more than Persephone ever has or ever will. Yet he was deprived of his greatest love and sent to live under the purple sun of Tartarus. How would that affect you? Hades was turned into a hardened god, yet inside he still grieves for the great loss he suffered because of his brother Zeus's pride.

Zeus, in response to his brother's pleading, unfeelingly said, "Be content. Though now you have no people in your kingdom, in time it shall be well-peopled. All who live shall in the end come your way. You have, moreover, in your keeping, all the vast wealth that lies hidden in the earth. You shall be the god of wealth; you shall be Pluto, the wealthy one!" (Herzberg, Max. *Myths and their Meaning*. Allyn and Bacon, Inc., pp. 152-153).

'Be content.' Easy for the Lord of the Universe to say.

Imagine Hades's delight when he sees a young maiden sitting under a tree, trying to keep dry in a thunderstorm. His hard heart melts as he hears her wishing for a place where it never rains, never hails, and essentially is the perfect paradise. And he knows just the place for her—the Elysian Fields! This is where the blest go, those who have never sinned. "Here fell not hail or rain or any snow nor ever winds blew loudly"

(Herzberg, p. 182).

Cautiously stepping closer, careful not to reveal his presence, he finds that it is Persephone, the daughter of his sister, Demeter. At first he thinks he ought not go to her because Demeter, whether she admits it or not, has a terrible temper. But poor Persephone looks so bored and wet and unhappy. So Hades approaches and says hello and tells her who he is and what he's thinking. At first she is a bit frightened, backing off and feeling wary. But then she stops and thinks, Why not? I'm not going to get an opportunity like this again, and I'm not going to be ruler or queen of anything else, so why not?

Now, we're used to the child inheriting his parents' things, whether it's money, land, or realm, but these are immortals. Her mother will not die. We're not talking about the daughter of a queen who will someday be a queen, in either the same or a different kingdom. This child will not get anything because she won't inherit anything. She won't be given anything by Zeus and the other gods, because she was born last. There's nothing left!

Hades and Persephone talk for a long while, and in the end they decide that Hades should talk to Zeus about it. Hades tries to talk Persephone into talking with her mother, too, but no, Demeter would never understand; she thinks her daughter should be happy the way she is, a girl eternally caught between childhood and adulthood. And who wouldn't be happy as the adored baby of Mt. Olympus? She gets to roam the planet, playing in field, forest, stream, and ocean, making daisy chains, flower crowns, and other such things. If they did go to Demeter, she would probably say that Hades had talked her into it, that it was just a phase she would grow out of. Then she would proceed to lock Persephone up in their palace for a long while until she was satisfied there would be no more talk of her dear brother. Agreeing that it would be futile, Hades and Persephone decide to meet again in two weeks.

Meanwhile, Hades goes to Zeus, saying that he wishes to marry Persephone. And who happens to be outside the door, eavesdropping, but Demeter! She thinks that this is some plot to make her beautiful Persephone as cold as he seems to be. This makes her so scared and so furious that she bursts into the room and screams that if Zeus allows this, she will personally make known to Hera all fifteen of his last flings.

What can the poor god say? Zeus tells Demeter to calm down, that maybe Persephone and Hades had actually fallen in love. Demeter then shrieks that if they had been together, which she was certain they hadn't, she would make sure they never were again. And with that, she stalks out.

Two weeks pass, and Hades meets a crushed Persephone, whose mother had come home raving about the nerve of Hades and warning her daughter to avoid him at all times. Hades, while listing the possibilities, mentions that they could elope. Persephone jumps up from the rock on which she has been sitting and throws her arms around his neck, saying that they would deal with her mother after they were married. A scene then takes place that could have come straight from a movie. The two climb into Hades's chariot and go riding off into the sunset, until the earth opens and swallows them in.

Upon their arrival at the gate to Hades, Hades announces that they will be going on a grand tour. Furthermore, he states that he refuses to be called Hades any longer, that from now on he wants to be called by one of his other names—either Pluto or Dis. Persephone decides on Pluto, then insists on him calling her Core, the pet name given to her by Zeus and her mother. They ride down the long passageway laughing, a sound rarely heard either in that hall or from Pluto's lips.

As they reach the Styx, the first of the five rivers marking the boundaries of Hades, they hear Cerberus barking. Persephone is frightened of the large, three-headed dog with a dragon's tail, but Pluto just laughs and says that he has given Ares the right to pet him, feed him, and throw stars for him to fetch and so Persephone should not be afraid.

Charon, the miserly old ferryman who takes dead folks across the Styx, grumbles when he sees the new queen, because he knows it's just going to mean more free rides across for gods and goddesses, which will cut down on the number of people he gets across, thereby lowering the amount of *oboli* he gets. Pluto and Persephone ride across, and Persephone comments on the dreadful color and odor of the river. Now she understands why an oath taken on this river by a god is never broken.

They pass the other four rivers: Lethe, the River of Forgetfulness; Acheron, the River of Woe; Phlegethon, the river that flows fire instead of water; and Cocytus, the River of Wailing. Persephone is beginning to have her doubts about living in this place for eternity, but she keeps silent, hoping that Pluto will show her something that will make it worthwhile. Pluto turns to her and tells her to close her eyes because they are approaching the palace.

He leads her to the middle of its courtyard and tells her to open her eyes. She looks around and tries not to look too dismayed, but Pluto can sense something anyway. It's a dark, gloomy place surrounded by foreboding dark trees; close by stretch meadows of asphodel, the lily of the dead.

Persephone turns to him and says, "Are these the flowers you were speaking of?"

Quickly Pluto answers, "No, of course not. Those are in Elysium; you'll see them later. Now let me show you to your room."

They walk to a beautiful suite where Persephone can see three women standing behind a curtain. Pluto announces that he has three servants to wait upon her. They step out from behind the curtain and Persephone gasps in horror. They are winged maidens with serpents twined in their hair and blood dripping from their eyes. Pluto sees her response and says that if she doesn't want them, they can go back to what they did before she came: pursuing those who escape punishment for the crimes they committed, and bothering them with all the horrors of a guilty conscience. Persephone quietly says that she would rather have her attendant from the surface, so Pluto dismisses the trio and goes to search for three gentlewomen willing to wait on his queen.

Persephone looks out only one window, having express orders not to look out the others. She sees people standing around, listless and blank. "That is the Field of Asphodel," she hears a voice say from behind her. She spins around and finds herself facing a mysterious Titaness. "I am Hecate, the goddess of witch-craft and sorcery. I managed to retain power after Zeus fought against Cronus. I send ghosts up to haunt the living. You were looking at the place where people are sent to wait for nothing, after they are judged, if they are found to be neither good nor bad. They are just dead. I expect I will be seeing more of you." And on that cheery note, Hecate disappears.

Just then, Hades returns with the earthside attendants. "Here they are, queens all three, I think. You'll be waited on royally. Now let's go see the paradise I promised you."

They walk out through the suite to a small courtyard. Surprisingly, it is bright and flowers are growing, and there is a fountain in the middle spouting clear water. Persephone starts to say how much she loves it, but Pluto cuts her off: "You think this is all? Go through the gate."

She does, and finds everything he had described to her—orchards of beautiful fruit, sports, dancing, singing—an endless bliss, just as he had promised her! Even warriors are resting, "their armor rusting, their chariots unused" (Herzberg, p. 182).

Endlessly she played here, dancing and singing along with the others, feasting and napping beneath the purple sun and shining stars. The only time she was torn away from this was when Hades requested her presence at a judgment or some other gathering. She sat upon her throne next to him, sometimes playing with the keys to the underworld or Pluto's magic staff, other times examining the writing on his trident or making crowns out of cypress branches. A few times she asked if she, too, could wear his cap of darkness, but the answer was always no. She wished she could be outside playing with the new friends she had made.

It was at one of these judgment sessions that Hermes found her. He came down and saw her bored; it seemed to him that she must always be so! Hermes demanded that in the name of Zeus she be returned to her mother.

The gardener overheard this, and, as just that day he had seen her eating out of a pomegranate, he leapt in and shrieked, "She has eaten at least six seeds. The law of the underworld is that she must stay."

By this time Persephone was crying because she would have to leave her happy life and go back to the boring existence she had led, doing the same things every day and avoiding mortals. Hermes took this as a sign that she was afraid she would have to stay, and was troubled, for he knew that she must remain if they were to uphold the laws.

Persephone prepared to visit her mother and tell her the truth. But when she and Hades actually arrived, Demeter ran out, grabbed her, and pulled her away; then she started screaming at Hades! What could poor Persephone do? To tell the truth now would be like exiling herself from her mother, which she didn't want to do.

So now the judgment is up to you. We know from the story of Orpheus and Eurydice how Orpheus convinced Pluto to let Eurydice go; it should be clear to us now that Pluto is not there to punish the dead. Said Museus, "Or bid the sound of Orpheus sing/Such notes as warbled to the string/Drew iron tears down Pluto's cheek/And made Hell grant what love did seek" (Herzberg, p. 187).

My client is not so cruel as to take a mother from

her daughter or, in this case, a daughter from her mother. All we ask is that, for each of the six seeds that the gardener saw Persephone eat, one month in Hades be granted her. The other six months may be spent with her mother. Thus will the laws above and the laws below be equally upheld, and the causes of both justice and love served.

ABOUT THE AUTHOR

Sarah-Scott Brett lives in Durham, North Carolina, and attends Riverside High School. She says she loves "anything involving water" and especially enjoys stream-walking in the mountains near her home. Computer role-playing, reading, and acting are also important to her.

You never forget your first mission.

The Mission

by BEN MILLER

Although I rarely get into trouble with my parents, as a young child I dabbled in the art of
mischief. I usually performed these miscreant
activities with my neighbor and comrade, Kyle. I will
always remember an incident that took place when we
were very young.

Kyle and I lived on a very small street. At the end
of the street stood a wire fence equipped with a makeshift
ladder. This fence represented our frontier, a barrier
that our parents forbade us to cross. Discovery by our
parents of passage over the fence meant certain death.

Beyond the fence was a huge field which stretched
out a few hundred yards to some complexes that made
up a Catholic high school. Behind the high school was
a small forest that, according to the older kids on our
block, contained a haunted graveyard. Past the forest
was a chain-link fence that bordered a road. And across
the road was Venture, a common department store.

Little did I know that I would never be able to set foot there again without remembering the fateful incident that took place one hot summer day.

It happened this way. Kyle and I had always been fans of GI Joe. Our games didn't actually consist of pure GI Joe hardware, but a combination of Mask and outdated Star Wars figures, complemented by an assortment of GI Joes, Joe's vehicles, and his plastic automatic weapons. We referred to all of the figures simply as our "dudes."

Anyway, we had this obsession with them. The game gave us godlike powers that allowed us to control our own world and decide the fate of anybody we chose. The game was our ticket to power. Spending a day at Kyle's wasn't complete without a GI Joe private war, after which all the fighters would once again become magically resurrected.

On the bad side were the Star Wars figures, and on the good side were the GI Joes. The Star Wars guys were always the enemies since they were only jointed at the hips and shoulders, and we preferred to play with the Joes, who were also jointed at the neck, knees, and elbows. The good side was led by Hawk, the Joe Commander. The bad side was led by the Cobra Commander, who was old and chipped. We were tired of him. There needed to be a new evil leader.

The Two Evil Twins had just come out in the stores, but they cost ten dollars. A three-dollar allowance meant only one new GI Joe character per week, and the last thing we were going to do was to save up to get the Twins. We couldn't go four weeks straight without a new Joe; we just couldn't accept the wait. We had a platoon of Joes, but we needed battalions, even whole armies of them. We had to expand and diversify our collection, and we weren't getting anywhere. Many months of frustration passed before we finally came up with an idea.

One day, as Kyle and I were controlling a village massacre in the woods behind my house, we came up with the plan.

"Hey, Kyle," I asked as I rolled a Cobra tank over a twig-woven fort, "how are we ever gonna get more dudes?"

"I don't know," he replied. "My dad won't raise my allowance."

"You don't need any more," I snorted. "You get five bucks. I only get three stupid dollars!"

"Yeah, but you don't hafta mow the lawn," he retorted as he positioned Barbecue on a tree branch. "I do."

"So how are we gonna get more dudes?"

"We could go to Venture and steal some."

"Steal some!" Frightening images of myself fleeing from wailing sirens in the dead of night pierced my mind. "You gotta be kiddin' me."

"You got any better ideas?" he said as he dropped Destro through a helicopter blade. He was right. It was probably the quickest way to get more Joes.

"Well, no," I said, still shaken by the thought. "But what if the police catch us?"

"Then we'll go to Death Row," he solemnly replied.

"Man, then my mom and dad would really be mad at me!" I said, cringing at the thought. "I'd probably get grounded for a month!"

"You couldn't get grounded because you'd get sent to the 'lectric chair."

"What happens when you get 'lectracuted in the 'lectric chair?" I asked, as I had Hawk throw Boba Fet off a tree branch and into a pit studded with sharp twigs.

"Well, first your skin burns and peels off. Then your eyeballs pop out. That's why they put a mask on you. So your eyeballs don't fall on the ground."

"What do they do with your eyeballs after they fall out?"

"I don't know. They probably put them in a jar and give them to your mom or an eye bank or something."

"Oh," I said, fascinated by the gore I was imagining.

"When my mom dies, she's going to get creenated and put in a jar."

"She's gonna get what?"

"Creenated. It's when you die, instead of getting buried in a coffin, they burn you in a fire until you're just ashes. Then you can keep them in a jar at home. And when you wake up and you miss her, you can say, 'Hi, Mom!' to her 'cause she's right there."

"But she's just ashes!" I exclaimed, perplexed by the idea.

"Right."

After contemplating for a few hours, I finally agreed to go to Venture with him. We packed some candy bars and a few Cokes and got on our bikes. We slowly rode them to the end of the street, where we hid them, well-camouflaged, in a nearby bush. Instead of climbing the ladder on the fence, we scooted through a dog-dug hole under the fence on our hands and knees.

We continued to stealthily crawl through the overgrown field. Then we ran across a school road and into a great, dark, and evil forest. Actually, it didn't even cover an acre, but this forest was different. In the center was the graveyard which we had heard terrible stories about and imagined held the corpses of great, evil kings. The truth about it that I learned when I was older was that it really held the bodies of 15 valedictorians who had wanted to be buried on school grounds.

"Man, this sure is spooky," I whispered.

Kyle and I prowled through the center of the graveyard and stopped short. There before us was a brand-new, gleaming, marble gravestone. In front of the stone was a fine blanket of newly uncovered earth.

"Oh my God!" I squeaked as our gazes met. Someone had actually died and was buried right in front of us! Memories of *Night of the Living Dead* flooded my mind as Kyle and I ran screaming through the woods, climbed over a chicken wire fence, and ran across a road as fast as our short little legs could carry us. We stopped at a telephone pole to catch our breath, wheezing so hard that one could have mistaken us for Lamaze students.

"I wonder if he got 'lectracuted?" I gasped, the adrenaline pounding in my temples.

"No. He was probably shot," Kyle returned, still gasping for air.

"I wonder if he—"

All of a sudden, I caught my breath. Realizing that we were in a parking lot, I tapped Kyle on the shoulder. Our eyes slowly looked upwards to fix on the dazzling black-and-white sign of Venture, gleaming in the sunlight.

Kyle and I slowly walked into the store. *Minimum security,* we thought, as our eyes scanned the place for

SWAT teams. We strolled into the toy section and to the back where the Joes were located. I cackled in delight as I spotted the Two Evil Twin Brothers staring down at me from the top shelf.

"Those twins cost ten bucks!" I snorted. "That's a total rip-off! Those guys who make them deserve to have them stolen. It's their own fault." Now I had justified my actions. In my mind, it was perfectly OK to take them.

"Right on, man!" Kyle said, as he ripped an eight-dollar Rambo figure from its package. I, too, ripped my treasure from its package, as we had planned, to decrease its bulk. Then we shoved our figures down our shorts and continued down the aisle. We began walking to the exit.

All of a sudden, I just about ran into the ample behind of old Mrs. Hobbes, our neighborhood gossip. At first I almost failed to recognize her because she was wearing her wig. Actually, she was almost completely bald underneath, and only took the wig off in and around her house, where Kyle and I often spied on her.

Disaster, I thought, as I alerted Kyle to the threat. Getting on our knees, we launched ourselves underneath the clothes rack to safety. Luckily, she hadn't noticed us. We got to our feet in the other aisle and headed for the exit. No one stopped us. We walked straight on through the sliding doors and into the parking lot. *Victory,* I thought.

My joy was suddenly cut short as a police car rolled in front of us. Fearful of being frisked, we scampered around the corner and hurled our merchandise into a ditch next to the lot where some construction had been going on. We proceeded to act as if we didn't notice the cop at all. The car slowed for a second and then moved on. We retrieved our treasures from the ditch and then began our journey home. It was an easy one.

Kyle and I celebrated our successful mission for two days. Then my mom got a phone call from Kyle's mother. Apparently, Kyle had buried the Rambo figure in his garden for safekeeping. Somehow his little brother, Ryan, had sniffed it out and dug it up. After hours of questioning from his mother, Kyle broke down and confessed his crime. Unfortunately for me, he blabbed. My parents interrogated me for a day before I finally gave up and admitted it, whereupon my dad drove me to Venture to return the Evil Twins to the manager. As we got out of the car, my dad hissed at me, "I'm going to be so mad if you go to jail, Ben!"

As we walked toward the automatic doors of Venture's entrance, a gut-wrenching knot formed in my churning stomach. What if I actually did get on Death Row? What if I had to go to the electric chair? I became dizzy. My mind swarmed within my head. What if my eyeballs really did pop out? I felt delirious. I could hardly walk straight.

All of a sudden, I just about stumbled into a gargantuan man in blue as my dad pulled me to a halt near the cash register. I looked up at a gigantic beast with a uniform on. Yes, it was a cop. The meanest cop I'd ever laid eyes on. He looked like a bulldog with a badge on. (I found out when I was older that he was really just a rent-a-cop, hired to deter thieves.) As I stood there, gasping for air and sweating bucketloads of grease, my dad nudged me forward.

"Go on, Ben. Tell 'im what you did."

Droplets of sweat streamed down my forehead and neck as I slowly stuck out my hand carrying the Evil Twins. "I took this," I squeaked.

"Hold on," the cop slobbered. "I'll get the manager."

Pretty soon the manager came. To my surprise, it was a nice lady. She took the Twins from my hand and said that it was OK since I brought them back, and refused to take any money from my dad. A feeling of relief washed over me as we left the store. I didn't have to go to jail! My muscles relaxed. Then I began to wonder about Kyle's fate.

Kyle, as it turned out, had been brought to the assistant manager, who was not so nice and demanded a fee of five dollars from his father. I never found out what actually happened to him that day. Kyle never really wanted to talk about it.

Kyle and I both received cruel and unusual punishments. I was grounded and couldn't ride my bike, watch television, or play with Kyle for two weeks. Kyle's punishment was that he was prohibited from playing with his GI Joe figures for the whole school year. Because Kyle owned the bulk of the collection, I, too, shared his pain.

Two years later, Kyle moved to Chicago. I rarely see him now, but when I do, we always recall our adventure together and all of our old memories come tumbling out. We're a lot older now, but once in a great while, secretly, I wish we could go back to those dark, cool woods behind my house and plan just one last mission.

ABOUT THE AUTHOR

Ben Miller lives in Kirkwood, Missouri, and is a student at John Burroughs School in St. Louis. Ben is active on his school's JV water polo team, plays violin in a youth orchestra, and has performed in a school musical. Other interests include hiking and wilderness activities.

Talking dogs, scrawny knights, and
daffy kings: Slapstick comes to Camelot.

The Questing Beast

by MATTHEW ROESSING

I can hear the barking of the dogs . . . Yes, the sound comes from that clump of bushes over there. Silently, I stalk my prey. A footprint here, a broken twig there, all these seemingly trivial details are vital to me. For the creature I am hunting is no meek deer or fawn. The animal I chase is the master of the hunt, and no animal in the world is more sly than he. My name is King Pellinore. My quarry is the Questing Beast.

I have pursued the Questing Beast, also called Glatisant, for many years, and yet he still eludes me. What is Glatisant? That answer is not easy to give, even by one such as I who knows him better than any man. Glatisant is a creature born to the hunt, a master of deception and trickery. What is his nature? To be hunted but never to be caught. How old is he? Glatisant is not a creature of time. My father hunted the Questing Beast, and his father before him, and on and on, from the Creation of Man. Glatisant is, was, and ever will be, and that is all I know.

You may ask how I, a mortal man, have managed to track such a magnificent animal for so long. The answer lies in the barking. That is the one fault of Glatisant which keeps him from escaping me forever. He has the sound of thirty hounds arising from his stomach. This noise is what finally reveals his hiding places.

Do not assume that this is a serious hunt on both parts. While I am intent on completing my quest, Glatisant finds the hunt a humorous game. He always plays this "game" fairly and doesn't even escape when I go to sleep each evening. In fact, many a night he has curled up near my fire, knowing that I would not capture him (for that would not be fair), and slept near my tent, the barking in his belly subsiding to a soft yipping that lulls us both to sleep. Then at dawn, he runs off into the woods, accompanied by the sound of hounds, with me close behind.

You may think that this is a strange way of life, but it is actually a quest followed by everyone in the world. For every man has his Questing Beast, an animal who runs ahead of him, one step out of reach, looking back and taunting him. For many, it is not an animal that they seek to subdue, but an emotion. Jealousy, Anger, Grief, Fear—these are all names of Questing Beasts. Some people capture their Questing Beasts and are troubled by them no more. Others chase theirs all their lives.

Am I to capture my Questing Beast, or am I destined to run after it for my whole life? Whatever fate has in store for me, I will not stand still while Glatisant slips through my fingers. I will track my Questing Beast to the ends of the earth, if necessary. This I vow.

The lone figure sat on horseback atop a solitary hill. It would be nice—and poetic—to say that his armor gleamed in the sunlight, the silver-gold rays of dawn glancing off his outstretched sword, as he sat on a beautiful midnight black charger. Yes, that would sound good, but it would also be a lie.

First of all, it was not dawn, but that time of afternoon when the sun beats down and the humidity is high, and everyone just wants to go home and sit in front of a large electric fan. This was quite a problem for the figure because, not only had electricity not yet been invented, but the horseman also had forty pounds of rather rusty armor to contend with. However, the figure continued to assume as knightly a stature as a 120-pound boy, sitting on a small, uninspired pony, waving a chipped sword, can muster. Every few moments he would consult a small, leather-bound book. It was entitled: *So You Want to Be a Hero—A Manual for the Would-be Protagonist.*

Perhaps a little background is needed for those readers who are thoroughly confused. The boy's name was Fenton. He came from a farm north of Portchester, Logres. Being so near to Camelot, he was brought up on stories of the bravery and chivalry of the Knights of the Round Table. He finally decided to leave his home and try to become a knight.

I am sure you have heard many stories like this one, where a young boy with noble blood takes up the hereditary sword passed down for centuries and goes to smite evil wherever it may lurk. This was Fenton's problem. He had no trace of noble blood, no years of dedicated jousting practice, and no hereditary sword. All he had was some rusty armor too big for him, a small pony that could never be mistaken for a noble steed, a chipped and dented sword, and the book, which he got free from the village merchant because no one else wanted it. With these prized possessions, he set off.

Enough background! Let's move to the present. After sitting on the hill waving his sword for about an hour, Fenton spied a passing knight who rode up to him and asked him what he thought he was doing. Fenton consulted his manual.

"Hold, recreant knight," he recited, "for I wouldst run a tilt with thee, truly."

"What?"

Fenton tried again. "I want to joust with you."

"Oh, OK."

They both rode their horses to the edge of the clearing and, without hesitation, charged furiously. It is at this point in most heroic fantasy stories that the young hero, despite enormous odds, smites his opponent to the ground. This is not always the case in real life, however, for Fenton caught his opponent's spear square on his helmet, flew off his horse, and landed on the ground with a loud *clank!* Fenton had had enough of this. He was hot, sweaty, and the fall hurt badly.

"It appears that you are no longer on horseback," the knight taunted. "Therefore, I will dismount, and let us fight with swords."

"Let's not," replied Fenton, getting on his pony and riding away. "I'm sick of being a hero. I'm going home."

And off he rode into the sunset.

And that's how it would have ended. That's how most stories like this one do end—with the hero riding off into the sunset. In fact, that's how I intended to end this story, but one character had different plans.

On his way home, Fenton became thirsty and stopped at a spring in the middle of the woods. Just as he dismounted, however, the noise of thirty hounds echoed through the forest. Fenton's pony, being rather skittish, took off through the trees. Just then, an animal with a lizard's head and a leopard's body burst out of a bush and pounced on Fenton. Yep, you guessed it—the Questing Beast! Tied to his tail was a long leash with a bewildered dog at the end of it.

"Help!" yelled Fenton.

Glatisant licked his face cheerfully, then bounded off into the forest, mentally laughing at me for thinking that I could get away with such an easy ending. The poor dog had no choice but to follow.

A few moments passed in which Fenton lay stunned on the ground; then a man popped out of the bushes.

"You, boy! Did a strange animal just pass by?"

"Uh . . . yes . . . I think."

"Well, tell me where he went!" the man exclaimed. "I must find him. That beastly Beast stole my dog!"

"Stole your dog, sir?" Fenton asked incredulously. "Does it eat dogs?"

"What?! No, of course not. He did it as a joke. Everything's a joke to that blasted animal. Well, anyway, what are you doing here? What's your name, boy? Stand up and answer!"

"Uh . . . sir . . ." Fenton ventured.

"Stand up, boy! What's wrong?"

"Sir, you're standing on my foot."

"Oh! So sorry."

Fenton carefully stood up.

"So, boy, what's your name and why are you here?" the man inquired.

"My name's Fenton, and I was going to become a hero, but I changed my mind and . . . Wait! Don't you have a beast to catch?"

"Oh, don't worry about Glatisant. He isn't going anywhere. My name's King Pellinore. Pleased to make your acquaintance."

"Your Majesty!" Fenton tried to bow gracefully but, due to the extraordinary weight of his armor, only succeeded in toppling to the ground.

"Oh, tut, tut!" exclaimed Pellinore, turning red. "You needn't bother with all that."

"But—" protested Fenton, trying to get up.

"Forget it!" cried the monarch, good-naturedly slapping Fenton on the back and pitching him forward again. "Now, where is that Beast? Glatisant! Yoo-hoo! I'm going home now, so you better come out!"

At this, the animal slunk out of the woods, still leading Pellinore's dog. The Questing Beast halted in front of Pellinore and looked at him slyly. The barking in Glatisant's belly had stopped.

"Why, Glatisant! Why aren't you barking? Really, this is most extraordinary!" exclaimed Pellinore, staring.

The Beast returned the stare with mischievous eyes, then spat a stream of water into Pellinore's face. Immediately, the barking returned. Glatisant, realizing that his barking stopped whenever he drank, had filled his mouth with water, enabling him to move silently.

"Why . . . you!" raged Pellinore, drawing his sword.

The Questing Beast amiably wound the dog's chain around Pellinore's legs.

"Hey! Knock it off! Stop it! Haaalp!" cried Pellinore as he lost his balance and tumbled to the earth, joining Fenton, who had been unsuccessful in his endeavors to get to his feet.

Glatisant barked with glee as he danced around his captives; then, tying them up with the leash, he carried them to Pellinore's castle.

Glatisant dumped them unceremoniously at Pellinore's door, then took off into the forest, leaving the two captives with the predicament of getting untied.

"Fenton?" called King Pellinore.

"Right here, sir!"

"Oh, I do wish you would stop calling me 'sir.' Can you reach the knife in my pocket?"

"No, sir. Your dog is sitting on me, sir."

"Oh. OK. Barney! Barney!" Pellinore yelled. The dog slowly got up off Fenton, walked over, and sat on Pellinore's chest.

"Stop it, you idiot! Get off!" shouted Pellinore. Barney licked his face.

"I've got the knife, sir!" Fenton exclaimed.

"Don't call me 'sir'!"

"Yes, sir—Oops! Sorry, sir . . . I mean . . ."

"Just shut up and untie me!"

"Yes, s— I mean, Pellinore."

"That's better," said the king, standing up. "Won't you come in?" Inside, Fenton told Pellinore about his adventures as a hero, while the king sat idly petting his dog who was attempting to eat the coffee table.

"So then I went into the forest and met you

and . . . What's this?" inquired Fenton, holding up a strange object that he had been sitting on. It was constructed of a few metal bars connected by a coil of the same material.

"Oh," explained Pellinore, "that was a birthday present from Merlyn. He's a real magician, you know. Why, I remember one time when he—"

"What is it?" asked Fenton, derailing Pellinore's train of thought.

"Hmm? Oh. Some futuristic device. Probably a mysterious icon of arcane knowledge which men were not meant to wot of," Pellinore explained. "Merlyn called it a Thigh Master."

"Wow!" Fenton exclaimed, impressed.

"Anyway, my boy, I grow tired of adventures. No more adventuring tonight! What I need is a good stiff drink." And with that, he led Fenton out the door.

The countryside had a certain quality of silence to it. It was not the sort of silence caused by the absence of sound, because the air was filled with the sound of crickets chirping, fireflies buzzing, frogs croaking, and a small, rainbow-colored parrot letting out an occasional squawk. Yes, you heard me right, but we'll get to that later. Now, where was I? Oh yes. This silence was like a blanket of peaceful sounds. But not all was quiet, because in this countryside there was a town. And in this town there was a tavern. And in this tavern was a table. And under this table was a man, his off-key voice raised in a song he couldn't quite remember the words to. Guess who?

Pellinore sat up and continued, "Mary had a . . .

a . . . a what? Hey, Fen . . . Fenton, whass the thing dat Mary had?"

Fenton tried to pretend that he didn't know Pellinore. Pellinore promptly passed out under the table. Since Fenton was the designated equestrian of the two, he was completely sober, as well as completely embarrassed at Pellinore's behavior. Incidentally, no one else in the tavern looked disapprovingly upon Pellinore's actions because they were doing more or less the same thing.

"I think we should be getting home now, Your Highness," Fenton hinted.

Pellinore said nothing. Fenton looked under the table.

"Bartender, I'll need a pitcher of water," Fenton sighed.

The bartender, a massive man with an even more massive stomach, brought over a pitcher. Fenton dumped it on Pellinore.

"Hey," remarked the monarch, waking up. "Wha . . . What are you doing?"

"Time to go home, Pellinore," Fenton explained.

"But we juss got 'ere!" Pellinore replied drunkenly.

All of a sudden the door opened and a lady walked in. Whistles and catcalls followed her to the bar.

"Are there any good knights in here who would help me?"

"Thass us," Pellinore called out. "Knights erat . . . eran . . . arrant . . . errant. Yeah, thass it! Errant."

The lady looked at him. "Anyone else?"

"Fair lady, my companion and I will serve you well, I assure you," Fenton said unconvincingly.

"Very well. I suppose you two will have to do. My

master's parrot has flown away, and I need knights to pursue it," she said, leading the pair out the door.

Pellinore looked at her suspiciously. "This wouldn't be an adventure, would it? We had a promise—"

"No, it's not an adventure," said Fenton knowingly. "It's a quest."

"Oh, a quest!" repeated Pellinore. He had reached the macho stage of inebriation. "That's different! Lead the way, young lady! Don't worry, I've handled quests much more difficult than this! Why, I remember one time when—"

"Here we are," interrupted the girl. "He's in here somewhere. Good luck!" And with that, she left them in the middle of a vast forest.

"Well, this was a brilliant idea of yours," snapped Pellinore after an hour of fruitless searching. He was sober now and wished he wasn't.

"My idea!" snorted Fenton. "You were the one who blurted out that we were knights!"

"Well, yes, but you accepted the quest!"

"I did nothing of the sort! I—" Fenton stopped abruptly, staring at Pellinore's hat.

"I say! Why are you staring at me like that?"

"Don't move, Pellinore! The . . . bird . . . It's on your hat!"

"Dear me! And it's a new hat, too!"

"Don't worry about the hat, Pellinore. Let's try to get the bird into this bag."

After several unsuccessful attempts to scrape the bird off Pellinore's hat, the two gave up.

"What are we supposed to do now?" whined Fenton.

"I know!" exclaimed Pellinore. "Let's take it to Merlyn!" He looked around carefully, then whispered conspiratorially, "He can talk to the animals, you know."

"What, like Doctor Doolittle?"

Merlyn walked around the frothing and bubbling cauldron, adding strange and bizarre ingredients as the ancient pot spilled clouds of purple steam. He muttered strange incantations under his breath—

"Skrow siht epoh i . . . Skrow siht epoh i . . ."

Then he pulled a teacup out of his mystic robe, dipped it in the mixture, and took a long, slow drink. He grimaced and walked over to a book resting on a table, its back cover facing the ceiling. Merlyn began leafing through the book backwards. He flipped by Sleep Potions, Love Potions, and Curse Drafts, then stopped on a page with a title of one word in heavy Gothic script: Coffee. He ran his finger down the list of ingredients.

"Sugar! Sugar—that's it! I forgot the sugar," he muttered.

Merlyn walked over to a shelf and picked up a bag marked Sugar. It was empty.

"Harry, I'm going out to get some more sugar. I'll be gone for a bit," Merlyn informed the large dog that was lying in the corner.

"Sure you are," Harry replied sarcastically. "You're going to have a secret meeting with Them, aren't you! I always knew you were a spy! But it will be to no avail! Our revolution will still succeed, and you lousy humans will be serving us soon!"

"Oh, calm down, Harry. I'm just going for a cup of sugar, and I don't understand what you have against humans anyway."

"You'll see. Justice will prevail!" growled Harry, as Merlyn walked out the door.

Fenton slashed at a branch that was blocking their way.

"I know his house is in here somewhere," murmured Pellinore.

The two travelers were pushing through a dense forest. The forest was pushing back at them with branches, brambles, and vines. So far, it was a clear victory for the forest. *Funny thing about roads*, Pellinore thought. *You never really appreciate them until they're gone.*

"Is this it?" asked Fenton.

And, indeed, it was. Merlyn's home was a thatched cottage with windows and shutters and the strangest lawn ornaments Fenton had ever seen. They were definitely not in the same class as pink flamingos and dwarves with fishing poles. If someone ran over one of these with a lawn mower, they'd risk rending the fabric of the entire universe!

Pellinore strode boldly to the door and knocked.

A voice boomed: "WHO DARES DISTURB THE DWELLING OF MERLYN, ARCHMAGUS OF ALL, CONQUEROR OF KINGDOMS, SUPREME WIZARD OF THE INFINITE DIMENSIONS? PLEASE LEAVE YOUR NAME AND MESSAGE AT THE TONE." *BEEP!*

"He must not be home," remarked Pellinore to the amazed Fenton. "Let's go inside."

Pellinore opened the door and walked in, the bird

still clinging to his hat. Fenton walked over to Harry and patted him on the head.

"Good boy. Nice dog."

Harry squinted at Fenton suspiciously. "You're one of Them, aren't you?"

Meanwhile, a group of men was meeting in a tavern near Pellinore's castle. They were large, serious men. They believed that all the power in the world should belong to them, and that they were right in getting rid of anyone who stood in their way. Their leader was a sadistic man who was the leader for just that reason. He had steely eyes, an intimidating squint, and a smile that had nothing to do with humor. A person had gotten between him and power, and he planned to remove that person, no matter what it took. They were meeting about Pellinore.

Fenton stumbled back, tripped over a table, and landed on the floor. "It, it talked!" he gasped.

"Oh yes," replied Pellinore. "That's Harry. Hello, Harry, old chap!"

Harry mumbled something about a conspiracy and then fell asleep.

Pellinore started browsing through the shelves. "Be careful around here," he warned. "Things aren't always as they seem."

Fenton nodded his agreement and sat down on a nearby sawhorse, which neighed in protest and walked stiffly away, leaving Fenton on the ground again. By now, Fenton wasn't surprised by anything. On a whim, he picked up a scrubbing brush and dropped it. One would have expected it to fall. It did not. Instead, it sprouted wings and flew out the window, shrieking, "I'm free, I'm free!" as it went.

Behind Fenton, Pellinore was testing various chemical solutions on his hat. Finally, one worked. Or, maybe you can say that it worked because the bird was no longer attached to Pellinore's hat. The reason for this is that Pellinore no longer had a hat. The bottle's label read: *Instante Disintegration Potione*. The hat had been quickly eaten away by the solution, and the bird had no choice but to step off. Pellinore, utilizing the amazing speed of thought and motion of the really desperate, grabbed a wire cage and stuffed the bird inside before it had time to react.

Mission accomplished, Pellinore succumbed to curiosity and began poking through the shelves. He grabbed a flask titled *Klophsky's Amazin' Detonatin' Potion*. Now, in those days, only a select few were literate, and King Pellinore was unfortunately not among them. In other words, he eagerly pulled out the stopper. *KABOOM!* Pellinore was thrown across the room as the sides of Merlyn's cottage collapsed into a heap of rubble. Pellinore was buried deep in what used to be shelving. Fenton spun around in horror.

"Oops," remarked Pellinore, surveying the wreckage.

Fenton dug him out, moaning, "We're dead now. Harry will tell and then . . ."

They both glanced at Harry. Harry dozed peacefully. If he was aware of what had taken place, it sure didn't show.

"So," said Fenton, "now what?"

Pellinore stood up. "We do the logical and intelligent thing under these circumstances."

"Which is?"

"We get the heck out of here before Merlyn comes home!"

"Good plan."

They walked out through what remained of the door.

The two returned triumphantly to the bar, carrying the parrot in its rusty cage. They entered the tavern to find . . . nothing! The establishment was completely empty, except for the bartender, who was attempting to clean one of the tables.

"Excuse me, sir," ventured Fenton.

"Yeah?" the bartender gruffly replied, then realized that they might be customers and said, "Yes?"

"Did you see the lady with whom we were chatting earlier?"

"Um . . ." Thinking was obviously a painful process for the bartender. "Nope, can't say as I did."

"What do we do now?" Fenton turned to Pellinore as the pair roamed the streets of the town.

Suddenly the parrot decided to speak. "*Squawk! Pellinore!*"

"Hmm . . ." remarked a flattered Pellinore, "maybe I'll just take the little rascal home with me!"

"*Squawk!* Pellinore!"

The men were sitting around a table, the more intelligent ones with their backs to the wall.

"He's a king!" one of them was saying. "He must have barrels of money."

"Not to mention rubies and diamonds," a second man put in.

"Yep," remarked their leader, "once he's out of the way, all his money and power will be mi—I mean, ours."

"Wait a minute," interjected one of the more sensible of the group. "Are we talking assassination here? We'll definitely get caught! It's not the kind of thing no one's going to notice."

"That's for sure," agreed the leader. "We'll just force him to leave the throne. How about a kidnapping? Does he have any relatives that he's extremely fond of?"

"Well . . . no . . . but . . ." answered one of the men uncomfortably. "But . . ."

"Come on. Spit it out!"

"Hesgotabeast."

"What?!"

"A Beast . . . The Questing Beast. It's an animal that he always hunts. It's pretty much his life."

"Hmm . . . It's worth a try. We'll kill this Beast then."

The meeting broke up as the members slipped away into the shadows.

Pellinore was lying on a velvet recliner back at the castle while Fenton was outside throwing horseshoes with the king's butler, Charles.

Suddenly a young boy burst into Pellinore's chamber. "Your Majesty!" he cried. "I have overheard terrible news!"

The boy told Pellinore of the odious plot against

Glatisant. It's amazing how, when confronted with a perilous situation, a person's character can totally flip around. Within minutes, Pellinore was armed and armored for battle.

"Kill my beast?" he sneered, a dangerous tone creeping into his voice. "We'll just see about that!"

At that very moment, the conspirators were in the forest, tracking their prey. However, this hunt was nothing like the playful romps of Pellinore and Glatisant, for these men had no honor and cheated to win. The men drugged the palace water fountain so that, after Glatisant took a drink, he began to slow down. The last thing he saw as he dropped off to sleep was a circle of men, closing in . . .

Pellinore raced through the woods, hacking and slashing his way through the brush. Racing, chasing, overtaking time itself.

The circle of killers drew closer, awaiting their signal to pounce.

Racing . . . racing . . . life and death hanging in the balance, for in this race there'd be no ribbon for second place.

The leader stepped into the circle, raised his dagger, and—A battle cry resounded through the forest as five hundred pounds of armored King Pellinore hurtled through the air, smashing full tilt into the leader and sending him sprawling. Pellinore rose over the leader's fallen body like a tsunami looming over Tokyo.

"All right," he said coldly. "Who else wants some?"

The men gawked at Pellinore, who stood there like a triumphant warlord. For a moment they wanted to run, but then their street smarts kicked in. They realized that they outnumbered the king ten to one. Pellinore looked around in despair. So far he had been driven by his rage, but now he was tired and doubted he could take down ten men.

Someone tapped one of the outlaws on the shoulder.

"Yes?" said the man, turning around.

Fenton's sword crashed down on the man's helmet, and the outlaw dropped to the earth, unconscious. Pellinore stood stunned while Fenton stormed through the crowd like a miniature typhoon. A huge warrior with a battle-ax confronted Fenton. Fenton kicked him in the shins, and the man fell down, clutching his leg and howling. Pellinore joined in the melee wholeheartedly, and the two fought back to back, driving off the brigands.

"*Aaaa!* Tree spirits! Tree spirits! Help us!" the kidnappers yelled as they scattered throughout the woods.

Pellinore strode over to the fallen leader and put his sword to the man's throat.

"Please, my lord . . . spare me!" the man pleaded.

"I've never killed a man in my life, and I certainly wouldn't start with the likes of you! Now, get off my land and don't come back!"

The man picked himself up and limped off. Pellinore, exhausted from battle, lay down next to Glatisant and fell asleep while Fenton kept watch. Glatisant raised his head, winked at Fenton, and slunk back into the woods. Fenton winked back.

Sometime later in the night, a bloodcurdling scream echoed through the forest. Merlyn had returned home.

ABOUT THE AUTHOR

Matthew Roessing lives in Springfield, Pennsylvania, and attends Archmere Academy in Claymont, Delaware. He submitted this story while at Drexel Hill School of the Holy Child in Drexel Hill, Pennsylvania. A fantasy and science fiction fan, he received a Young Authors of Delaware County Award for his fiction. Besides reading and writing, Matthew's interests include drama and musicals, juggling, camping and hiking, tennis, golf, archery, and soccer.

They were forever friends.

It Rained for Stevie

by Jodi Zislis

The sun rested on the horizon, its golden glow shining on Stevie's face. The summer's air was warm and the breeze smelled of rain, as if there was going to be a storm. Her family had been back from David's funeral for four hours. They had changed out of their dressy, dark-colored clothes and silently went on about their business. Stevie still wore her black dress which by now had become wrinkled. She gently rocked on her back porch swing; she'd been sitting there since they had come home. Her cheeks sparkled in the fading sun from freshly cried tears. Big, salty droplets fell from her face onto her dress.

The back of Stevie's house faced a huge field whose yellowing grasses swayed in the breeze all the way out to the horizon. The field that Stevie's house overlooked was just off a big, steep hill. Stevie loved where she lived because her family had the entire hill and field all to themselves. She lived in an ordinary neighborhood with friends, a school, and a grocery store, but because they were out in the country, everything was spread out a little more. Stevie's neighbors were close enough, however, that she could hear them laughing as they played a game of kickball near her house. She wondered bitterly how anyone could be laughing on this miserable day.

Just as Stevie was changing positions on the swing because her leg had fallen asleep, her mother came out to invite her in to dinner. She was a tall, graceful woman whose step was so light that she had often startled people by suddenly appearing behind them. She approached Stevie, a worried expression on her tired face. She gently placed her slender hand on Stevie's shoulder from behind and said softly, "When your Grandpa Joe died, for a whole year I just wasn't sure I could go on living without my father. Then for another year I still cried sometimes."

Stevie knew her mother was trying to comfort her, but she also felt that her efforts were useless. Stevie rolled her teary eyes and looked in another direction.

Her mother went on, "I know exactly what you're going through, Stephanie." (It wasn't often that her mom called her by her given name.) "It's all right to feel sad. I know that David was an important part of your life. And the best thing to do when—"

"Mom," Stevie interrupted. It wasn't that Stevie wasn't interested, but she wasn't in the mood for talking. She just wanted to be alone. Her mother caught the hint of impatience in her daughter's voice.

"Do come in and have a bite to eat. You haven't eaten in two days. Aren't you hungry?"

Stevie just shook her head and wished her mother

would go back inside.

"But a growing fourteen-year-old girl like you needs her—"

Stevie shook her head again, more firmly this time. Her mother got the picture. She hadn't meant to nag. She knew what a sensitive time this would be for her daughter and was not hurt by Stevie's attitude toward her. She remembered well the many hours she herself had spent alone when her father died.

Stevie was relieved to hear the screen door closing behind her mother. She was alone again. She had never really considered herself alone before because she had always counted on David to be there for her when she needed someone. But now she was alone for real. David had left her that way. The pain in her heart was greater than it had ever been since things with David had started to go downhill. Stevie never had to deal with such a serious tragedy before except when her dog died, but that could hardly compare to the loss of the closest friend she had ever had. Nothing had ever hurt this much.

She closed her sad green eyes as another big teardrop rolled down her cheek and tumbled to her dress. She clearly remembered the last things she had done with David. The memories flooded through her mind as if they had just happened.

David was beautiful. His sunlit chestnut hair always fell in his eyes when he ran. He had huge, curious hazel eyes always looking for new things. He was good in almost every sport but was best at running. David was fast. Stevie, among others, admired him and would trade nearly anything to be as swift as David. Because he ran frequently, he had developed a solid build. He had always been the adventurous, daring type; this made him fun to be with. His easygoing style and great sense of humor added to his lovableness. Stevie knew that there was no such thing as a perfect person, but if someone had to be it, David was definitely the one. He was the best friend she'd ever had, and he had been for a long time, ever since the two of them were three years old.

"Let's go!" one of them would always shout as they flew down the hill to race. They raced each other nearly every day. David almost always won, most of the time by a long shot. Occasionally he would purposely stumble to give Stevie a chance to catch up. Then she would win, and although she knew she hadn't won fairly, she still felt good. At first, Stevie felt awkward about running against David, but she soon got over the feeling.

When they were very young, neither of them could understand how there could be a place they could see but not get to. This place was the horizon. Nearly every time they'd race, they were determined to have the horizon be their finish line. They would stand behind a stick-drawn line in the dirt, then on the shout of "Go!" they'd run. Stevie always ran hard and fast. She'd give it her all, but it just wasn't enough to get past David's swift stride. They'd run and run, but each time they would get to about the place where they thought the horizon should be, they'd find it still that much ahead of them. The two of them would fall down in the golden field, exhausted.

Then there'd be days for staying indoors, when the sky was gray and the air was cold. Stevie could still

see those raindrops, dribbling down the window outside. The wind blew hard, and every now and then
the two of them could hear a soft rumbling of thun-
der in the distance. She and David both loved the rain
and the fresh clean scent it always left behind. Stevie
was sprawled on her sofa and David sat in an old, over-
stuffed chair with his feet propped up on the arm of
the couch. The weather made them feel lazy and they
decided to spend the afternoon occupying themselves
with doing nothing. So they spent the day wasting time,
watching old movies on the VCR, eating popcorn, watching raindrops race to the bottom of the windowpane,
and wasting more time. They always managed to have
so much fun, no matter what they were doing, as long
as they were together.

The roads had dried from the rain the day before,
and a bright, sunny, fresh new day was beginning. Stevie
had arrived at David's house around midafternoon.

"Do you wanna watch the late show tonight?" he
asked her enthusiastically. (David was always enthusi-
astic.) "That is," he added, "if you can stay up!"

Stevie knew he was joking, but just for the heck of
it she said, "I bet I can stay up longer than you!"

"So, is it a bet?" he asked.

"Yup. It's a bet!" Stevie confirmed, and they shook
hands on it and laughed.

That night they took their sleeping bags and met
in the field behind Stevie's house. The plan was that
they were going to stay up all night to prove to each
other who could stay up the longest. And that's exactly what they did. They joked and laughed and talked
all night, telling ghost stories and jokes, and remembering the fun times they had had together. Then they

would laugh some more. The air was warm all night, and the field was silent and peaceful. The two of them had the night all to themselves.

As the white sun peeked slightly over the edge of the field, Stevie sat up and rubbed the sleep from her eyes. For an instant she'd forgotten where she was. She looked about her and saw the vast field. To her left was David's back. They had both fallen asleep, and now the rising sun had awakened Stevie.

Before waking David, she sat for a few minutes looking around her. Everything sparkled from beads of dew that had magically appeared in the night. The stillness of that morning gave Stevie a special feeling. It's the same feeling you get when you look out your window the morning after the first snowfall, before there are footprints or sled tracks, when none of the icicles have broken and everything glistens with a picture-perfect glow. That's how she felt.

Stevie nudged David with her elbow and he mumbled, "Not yet, Mom. Just a few more minutes." Then he sat up and remembered what he was doing there. "Oh!" he said, embarrassed.

"So who won?" Stevie asked, remembering their contest.

"I dunno," he answered as he tried to smooth down his hair. They sat up side by side and, silhouetted against the bright sky, looked into the sunrise.

Trying to make conversation, David said, "Tell me a secret."

"What secret?" Stevie asked, totally bewildered by his odd request.

"Any secret," he answered.

"OK," she said. "You can't tell anybody, though,

OK?"

David nodded hastily.

"I have seven pairs of green underwear!" she said. They burst out laughing.

"No, really," she said, trying to stop laughing. Then, after a moment of thought, "I wish that no matter what happens . . . no matter what . . . we'll always be very best friends forever and ever." Stevie paused and then added, "Now you tell me one."

David thought for a second and said, "OK. Since we're gonna be best friends forever, you gotta promise me this. If I die first, you won't forget me—"

"David!" Stevie interrupted, flustered. "How could you say that?!"

"Just listen, then promise. You won't forget me and you gotta promise that when I die you won't be sad. I could never leave you. I NEVER will," he promised.

Stevie wasn't sure that he was making sense, but he sounded so sincere. She honestly believed him. She was silent for a second. "I promise," she said. "And the same goes for me."

They smiled at each other as they gathered their sleeping gear silently. The sky became radiant as the sun continued to rise. They walked up the hill to Stevie's house, where a steamily delicious breakfast of pancakes awaited them. As Stevie ate, she tried to make some sense out of what David had said.

A few days later, David was supposed to come over and watch the baseball game with her on TV. It had already begun. Stevie began to pace, nervously glancing out her window each time she passed. She tried to sit down and just relax, but couldn't. She knew David would call if something was wrong. This wasn't at all like him. About fifteen minutes later the telephone rang. It was David.

"I'm really, really sorry. I'm calling from the doctor's office. I just forgot to tell you about my appointment. I'm really sorry. Tell me who wins, OK?" He hoped she would not be upset.

"No problem," Stevie said, trying to cover her disappointment. She plopped back down on the couch and gloomily watched the baseball game alone.

"Ready . . . set . . . GO!!" Stevie shouted as they ran through the field toward the finish line two weeks later. Stevie won for the second time in a row against David.

"Come on," Stevie said. "Three out of five!" She was suddenly filled with great confidence from her victories.

"OK," David agreed, panting for air. They began to race again, and after a few yards David dropped back tremendously. Stevie stopped in her tracks and turned around to find David hunched over and gasping for air. She had never seen him do such a thing.

"Are you all right?"

"Fine," he replied. "Just out of breath."

Stevie knew David didn't get tired that fast. He could run four or five races before getting winded. Something was definitely wrong. But Stevie didn't say anything more about it.

Stevie began to see less and less of David, but she worried more and more about him. As the month dragged on, David seemed to grow weaker and weaker. They stopped racing and nearly stopped even seeing each other because David was constantly at doctor appointments. And there were so many of them, one right after another! When Stevie and David were together, they would spend their time playing board games and things like that. David, who had always been smiling, smiled much less. Everything used to get a flash of his pearly whites, but not anymore. Stevie watched an enormous transformation take place in David over that month. It was especially sad to see the smiles disappear.

They pretty much kept the problem to themselves until one day, when Stevie just couldn't stand it anymore. She decided to take action. As David was returning home from another doctor appointment, he found Stevie sitting on his front steps waiting for him. She stood as he approached her and took his arm, steering him in another direction.

"We've gotta talk," she said softly. They walked in silence for quite some time, side by side, their shadows leading the way, before Stevie broke the horrible sound of quiet.

"What is going on?" she said in a frustrated tone. It was clear what she was talking about. When David did not answer, Stevie didn't ask twice. She knew that he would answer when he was ready. He suddenly stopped walking and looked Stevie right in the eye.

"They tell me I have cutis anserina."

"Cute . . . what?"

"Cutis anserina," he repeated.

"What on earth is that?!"

"It's . . . GOOSE BUMPS!!!"

They began to laugh. But Stevie knew it wasn't true. She was glad that he hadn't lost his touch. He could still make her laugh. She loved to laugh with David. But when she wiped the smile from her face, David knew he had to tell her.

"I have cancer," he said softly. The tone of his voice let Stevie know that this time it was no joke. She desperately searched for some humor in his face but found none. A horrible pang of panic shot through her body like a bolt of lightning. She felt her knees turn to jelly and her jaw dropped. Stevie could feel her heart swimming in her shoes. She felt as if she had just been slapped in the face. "Oh my God" was all she could manage to say.

One day while they were quietly playing a game of Monopoly, Stevie asked David, "Do you ever think about dying?" He rolled the dice and moved his game piece before giving his simple reply.

"Yes."

"A lot?"

"Yes."

"Are you afraid?" Stevie wanted to know.

"Yes."

"Me too," she said softly. She looked at the board to see where David's piece had landed. "You owe me twenty-six dollars rent," she told him in the same gentle tone. They smiled at each other as he handed Stevie the colored paper.

"What do you think will happen to me?" David asked her.

"I wish I knew. Would you visit me?"

"All the time!" His smile was so relieving. They decided that they weren't in the mood to play anymore. Instead, David requested a hug from Stevie. She was glad that they were not afraid to talk about it with each other. So was David.

Three more weeks went by before David was rushed to the hospital. His mother had called and asked Stevie to come immediately at David's request.

As soon as Stevie arrived, she flew to his side. His face was so pale and there were so many tubes hooked up to him and so many machines, it was scary. David looked so sad. She took his hand in hers and fought to hold back her tears, but she no longer could. They rushed down her cheeks as the raindrops had raced down her windowpane. She was petrified. David was going to die, and she was going to sit there watching. A sudden burst of fury shot through her as she realized that the very best friend she'd ever had was dying in front of her and there was nothing she could do to stop it. She could not pretend that it wasn't happening. She clung to David's hand, squeezing harder, as if holding on to him physically could hold him back from dying.

"No," she whispered to the helpless figure on the stiff hospital bed. "I won't let you go!" She gritted her teeth in determination and squeezed his hand even harder.

David said so softly, "Come here." Stevie bent over so that her ear was right by his face. He whispered into her hair, "Stevie, I have to go now. Do you remember when we told secrets in the field? I still promise what I said. I will NEVER leave you."

"I don't understand," Stevie whispered.

"Not in body, but in mind," he continued softly, ". . . in heart . . . in soul. You know how we love the rain. The next time it rains . . . then you will see me. I love you, Stevie . . . I will be seeing you . . . Then we'll race for our two . . . out of . . . three . . ."

The tears were streaming down so fast. Her sobs were muffled as she held her free hand tightly over her mouth in disbelief at what was happening. She was crying so hard that she couldn't breathe. Without letting go of his hand, she looked up and realized for the first time that David's mom was kneeling at his other side and his father was standing beside her. To Stevie everything was blurred through her tears. She looked back at David, praying that when she did he would be smiling up at her, saying it was all a mistake.

David opened his eyes and looked at Stevie. He gently squeezed her hand and tried his hardest to smile one last time for her. Then his grip loosened from around her hand, and he closed his eyes again.

"NOOOOOOOOO!!" Stevie cried out.

But David could not hear her. The jagged jumping zigzag on the heart monitor had become one horizontal line that ran endlessly across the screen. After a few minutes, Stevie carefully laid David's hand at his side, bent over him, and ever-so-gently swept a kiss across his cheek.

"Thank you," Stevie whispered. "Nobody could have been a better friend. Nobody . . . " her voice trailed off. David looked so peaceful. She gently pushed his bangs out of his eyes, stood up, and walked out of the room.

The sun had almost completely sunk below the horizon. Stevie stirred on her back porch swing.

Raindrops had fallen from the gray clouds, and a gentle misty fog had settled just above the ground.

Stevie wiped her eyes with the back of her hand and looked out over the field. Her field . . . where they'd raced, and told secrets, and laughed. It had belonged to them.

Stevie noticed the raindrops beginning to fall more and more rapidly as they splattered the ground. And all at once, for the first time since David had died three days ago, she smiled. Remembering David's words, Stevie rose from the swing and stepped out into the rain. It was coming down gently and had that wonderful fresh scent. She smiled wider and wider until she began to laugh with joy. The tears on her face mingled with the rain. Stevie was really seeing David, laughing with him! A load of a hundred tons was lifted from her shoulders. She could see him smiling at her for the first time in so long. Stevie cried out to the sky, "I'm so glad that you're here!" and ran down the hill to the field. She ran swiftly, her black dress flapping in the breeze. With a sudden burst of energy, she raced three times, then fell exhausted in the wet grass. She hadn't run in such a long time. It felt so good.

"There!" she yelled, looking up. "You won! Two out of three!" She smiled and laughed as the rain sprinkled her face. She suddenly felt so strong and free that she could have flown to the horizon in no time at all.

ABOUT THE AUTHOR

Jodi Zislis lives in Columbia, Maryland, where she attends Oakland Hills High School. She has acted since age five, and now is involved in Onstage Productions, a local theater company. She paints, writes poetry, and has designed award-winning posters on crime prevention and fair housing. Jodi began writing "It Rained for Stevie" while at Owen Brown Middle School.

The burning colors of madness . . .

Starry Night

by MATTHEW CHENEY

Vincent van Gogh is dead. And I am alive. I, Vincent's spectral self, am alive, and always will be. I was supposed to cultivate his genius and make the world aware of it so that he would become famous for eternity and I would become one of the Great Ones. But I have failed. I did my best, but Vincent let himself go mad. The fool killed himself far too early, and now I must wander the halls of the past because the Great Ones feel that I have failed. It's all Vincent's fault! He has deprived me of eternal pleasure, and I shall always hate him for it.

But you do not need to know any of this.

Arles. Arles, his place of madness. The children would run around him when he journeyed outside. They would throw pebbles and dirt and chant, "The Madman of Arles, the Madman of Arles, he is the Madman of Arles!"

The adults were afraid of him. Afraid that he would do something beyond reason, something that they could not even imagine. They didn't know what he'd do, but they were convinced that he would do it.

So they had us locked away. Then we came back. But then that stupid fool Vincent went back on his own. And back and back and back and back, until his mind was pummeled into the outer reaches of an insanity he yearned for. He thought insanity would bring him freedom. Then one horrible Sunday, he was painting in a wheat field. He took out a revolver and shot himself in the chest. He staggered back home and up to our room, where I was waiting. He collapsed onto the floor. "You idiot!" I said. "You poor, stupid fool! We had so far to go, yet you could not hold on!"

"Help me up onto the bed," he pleaded quietly, as if he had not heard me. I stared at him. He knew I was disgusted that he had let himself become a slave to frustration. "Please help me." He struggled to pull himself up and onto the bed. Blood was falling to the floor, saturating his shirt, staining the white sheets. I cursed him and still curse him. I hated him and wished he would just die. But he held on until Tuesday, as if spiting me. I wanted him to suffer, but he was immersed in insanity and loving every minute. Finally he succumbed to a death he had been courting for ten years.

But I am getting ahead of myself. I want to speak about one night in Arles, five years before Vincent killed himself.

We were sitting in our room, Vincent looking out the window, studying the sky. It was alive, amazingly alive! The clouds churned and broke like waves. The moon, a brilliant crescent, radiated and lit the colors of the sky on fire. The stars were bullet holes randomly shot into the burning blues. And I could see Vincent imagining the town burning, and a great cypress standing tall, growing, as all other life died.

Then he got up and walked outside and down into the town. I followed him. Vincent would look up occasionally and glance at the sky. He stared at the moon and imagined it engulfing all of the world. We walked on.

He looked up again as we reached town. For a moment we both saw that the sky was alive, rolling and tumbling like apples in a barrel pushed down a hill, but it was all Vincent's imagination.

We walked into the small church. Its steeple was the tallest point in town, and Vincent yearned to be in it. So we found our way up. The view was unlike any he had seen before. To a normal man it would have been merely beautiful, but to Vincent it was a masterpiece of light and hues. He studied every ripple, every flow of shadow, every ray of light. To him form was light and darkness and color, and these were the things he imprinted on the canvas of his mind.

And then all at once it happened. It was a dream for him, a nightmare for me.

This was not a normal night by any man's conception of normality. No, Vincent and I had both seen the impossibility of such beauty and perfection. Now it was time to see it as it was. We would enter into it. We would not hold back.

It started with Vincent falling to the cold wood floor. And there he dreamed, or thought he dreamed, but I knew better.

He fell through his own mind. He cascaded through the multitude of memories, the shards of the past that he had collected since he was born. And he landed at the bottom of a long, dark tunnel. The darkness itself had lines—brush strokes to Vincent. He let himself be enveloped by them. And then he saw it all, his own painting. It was revealed to him how to make every brush stroke count, every molecule of paint. It was revealed to him how to make his every emotion burn through the canvas. And then the reality of life was revealed to him. The true reason. It scared him. But he awoke.

I know now what this vision was, though I didn't know then. I only knew that Vincent was failing and that my job was to try to make his genius work. But if Vincent was failing, then I was failing, and if I failed, then I could never be a Great One. So that night, in an act of desperation, my subconscious powers seized hold of Vincent's world and his potential genius and lifted his vision above that of the mortal, of the ordinary artist. He saw wonderful, beautiful secrets. His genius was awakened.

He worked harder every day. He painted himself into the canvas. He used the palette knife to glue gobs of color to the canvas, to practically sculpt the painting. He never knew what he was doing from then on— he just did it. I know this.

Frequently he dreamed of my world. At first it disturbed me, but it shouldn't have. I wanted him to have every chance to pierce the Unreality, our world beyond.

He saw his canvases burning into the eyes of people, pulling them in and grinding their selves to shreds.

He smiled. I showed him clouds and planets and colors beyond his conception. It made him suck his air in and open his eyes.

The mornings were the greatest times for him. He would sit at his easel and paint away and away and away, and soon would come power. No longer was shape shape; shape became color and light. No longer was color color; color became the blood of the painting. No longer was the brush a brush; a brush became a sword brandished against the blankness of the world he knew and lived in. He learned to explode everything so that true form was revealed. He saw like few before him. He saw what very few mortals have seen, something censored by culture and community and people. The people—self-proclaimed experts and blind automatons—then scoffed at him, because they were fixed in their reality. He did not show what they wanted to see—the static, the safe, the predictable.

But Vincent—Vincent the fool!—didn't know that. He'd caged himself in his color and his light and his form and his canvas. We could have been successful. Did Picasso give up? No! But he didn't know of Picasso. Did Leonardo give up? Did Michelangelo? Did Renoir, for that matter? Damn Vincent! Damn his foolishness and his genius! Pure, unfiltered genius finally poured from him. And that is what the Great Ones saw in him. And that is why They entrusted him to me.

I remember a Saturday night. It was dark, very dark, without clouds or color. Vincent was headed toward the brink. He smiled constantly and talked to walls. True, he still talked to me, and everyone thought that was insanity, but then he started the business with the walls. He would talk with them for hours. And I would sit back and cry and cry. Why couldn't he just grab hold of his sanity and become a sane genius again?

But this Saturday night he was his old self. He was quiet, yes, very, and I couldn't detect any irrational disturbances in his mind, so he was better than usual.

He looked out the window at the darkness and shook his head. "It is bad, very bad, Emille (he called me Emille, for some mad reason known only to him). It is like evil struts across the night. It is—never mind . . . it doesn't matter."

"Certainly it matters, Vincent. Everything matters. What is it?"

"It is terrible, is what it is. I wish so much that on nights when I am sane the nights could be beautiful. God knows that all the other nights are black. Always. Even the days are black."

He was babbling, but through his babbling I could detect true yearning for something that he hadn't had in years. He wanted the nights to be beautiful, like his dreams and his paintings. The insanity blocked what little beauty there was for him.

"Vincent, do you remember a few years ago—in the town? Do you remember that sky? Do you remember what you saw?"

His gaze fell downward, and the shadows shifted. He whispered, "Yes."

"Can you see it, Vincent?"

His hands touched the window. He stood up. "Yes. Yes. Yes! I see it!"

I peered into his mind and the image was there. But slowly it was transforming into something differ-

ent. It was becoming less polished. It was puffing out—
trying to become three-dimensional on a two-dimen-
sional surface. Light was twisting; the stars and moon
were exploding. The clouds rolled along like phantom
carriages, twisting the blue darkness with them. The
town was enveloped by the umbrage. And the great
cypress stood strong against the nocturnal world. This
was Vincent's night, throbbing in oils. Nothing more
brilliant had come from his mind before.

"Vincent . . ." My words were made of weakness,
for I didn't know what to say. "Vincent . . . it is . . .
beautiful . . ." *Beautiful* was too feeble a word to describe what I had seen. I had no words for what I had
seen.

Vincent sat before the window, dreaming of the
starry night years before.

He began work the next morning. The people were
concerned by his sudden, invincible obsession. He had
been calm, painting with ease, with a brush and not a
palette knife. But now he was working with ferocity.
Three canvases were thrown out when he deemed
them imperfect. "I can't do it, Emille. I know what it
should look like, but the brushes and knife are tools
that will never work. I need something flexible. Something that will bend with the colors and light. Something magical."

"Test things, Vincent. Something will work."

So he tried leaves, grass, twigs, rocks, cloths, glass,
dirt, his own fingers. Finally, after testing them all, he
combined them. He ended up using brush and knife
for the broad strokes, but details that only he could

see were painted over with other tools.

His starry night was captured. It drove him totally insane, but it was captured. It was a self-portrait of Vincent's mind, disguised, and there was no escaping it.

He painted nothing of such genius before or after. It wasn't his last, for he puttered about and produced some lesser works afterward, but it might as well have been his last. He had exhausted his power, used it up.

On a Sunday a year later, Vincent threw his brush into the wheat field and took a revolver and shot himself in the chest. He was frustrated by the world's failure to appreciate him, and he was a prisoner of his own insanity. I told him he was a fool, that we had years and years of genius ahead of us, but he wouldn't listen.

Now the story of the starry night is told.

Vincent may rest in peace, and I may wander more calmly. Whether you believe or not is of no concern to me; I have released my burden, released myself.

I wish that Vincent could see the world today—the stars and sky and trees are as alive as ever.

*

ABOUT THE AUTHOR

Matthew Cheney lives in Plymouth, New Hampshire, and attends the New Hampton School, in New Hampton. He considers this story about Vincent van Gogh "historical fantasy . . . I asked myself what was underneath van Gogh's madness, and I found a person (actually a spirit) that controlled him. There, along with some strange visions of his Starry Night, *was my fantasy coming alive."*

A Scotland Yard tale of lies, greed, and deception . . .

The Chief Inspector

by KATHERINE STANLEY

M r. Dinkins? Mr. Dinkins, sir? It's Inspector Griggs, sir, come to ask you a question. 'Ave you the time?"

After a brisk invitation to enter, Griggs tentatively pushed open the door. He was a tall, gangly young man with a budding beard and, at the moment, shaky knees. He'd graduated from officer training six years ago and been remarkably successful working his way up through the ranks at Scotland Yard; however, he'd never met the Chief Inspector, at least not to discuss a case. He scratched his beard and looked with some awe at the small figure sitting behind the desk in the crowded office.

The Chief Inspector glanced at the newcomer through his round glasses and set down his pen. "Well, Griggs?" he inquired when it was evident that the young inspector was tongue-tied. "What is it that you want?"

Griggs hurriedly took a seat in one of the glossy

leather chairs and opened a folder. "Well, sir," he began, hoping that his voice was not sounding as uncultured and shaky as it seemed to him, "it's like this. You did a case a while back—when you was an inspector, sir—and it's 'aving some reoccurrencies, as you might say. And I says: I'll go and see the Chief Inspector, since 'e knows most about this perticular case, and you see if 'e won't straighten it all out."

"And," said the Chief Inspector, "what case might this be that is giving you such trouble?"

"Oh!" said Griggs, embarrassed at having omitted such an important detail. "I am sorry, sir. Let me see . . . yes, it was at an 'otel in Rumford. Involved the murder of a Mrs. 'umphries."

There was a silence and then a nod of recognition. "Oh, of course, of course," said the Chief Inspector. "I remember the Humphries case quite well. I came upon it quite by accident, you know, but it was lucky that I did, since that was the case that gave me my promotion. The Rumford Inn. A strange little place . . . I wonder if LeClair ever got over the shock . . ." And, folding his pale hands over his knee, he lapsed into remembrance.

Inspector Joseph Dinkins wiped his lips and breathed a sigh of contentment. It had been a hard day, with his motor breaking down, the long stretch of road he had had to walk for an auto mechanic, and the bumpy ride to the hotel with the Egyptian taxi driver. But, Dinkins thought, a steak and kidney pudding, nicely done, can put everything right. After spending a few distasteful moments waiting for the bill and watching a potbellied American devour a steak with all the delicacy of a hungry Labrador puppy, he strolled out of the small hotel's restaurant.

Dinkins was a retiring man: his quick, precise walk and impeccable dress made one feel that to talk to him uninvited would be to throw his whole life off course, as would introducing foreign matter into a perfectly balanced machine. However, he had his share of human curiosity, and when he found himself in a room called "The Red Lounge" (as a clumsily made sign over the door proudly proclaimed), he adjusted his spectacles to examine his fellow occupants.

He decided they were a mostly uninteresting bunch. Besides the girl in the window seat with bright red nail polish and, Dinkins thought, rather nice legs, there included only a plump woman intent on some sort of knitting journal, a man in a rather ugly green tweed suit who was examining one of the old books on the shelf, and, strolling in, the meaty man from the restaurant.

An article in the *London Times* was about to engage Dinkins's attention when it was drawn away by the sudden entrance of a small, dumpy woman wearing a large black hat and, it seemed, several hundred bracelets—followed by a maid with a dust cloth. The woman sat down on the sofa next to the American and began to sift nervously through the handbag on her lap. It was several seconds before she seemed to realize there was anyone else in the room. She looked, with a surprisingly penetrating gaze, at each curious face in turn. Then her hesitant smile turned into a slack drop as if she had just remembered something. With a scream, she fainted onto the rug.

She was revived with someone's smelling salts. No explanation was offered for the woman's sudden weakness, and when she retired to her room in her hurried, fearful way, the curious witnesses settled back into their reading and contrived to put it out of their minds. But still they wondered and worried.

An otherwise uneventful evening blended into night. Then came the pale gray light of dawn, seeping in from beneath the heavy curtains. Suddenly Dinkins jumped up, snapped on the bedside light, and tied the sash to his bathrobe in haste. Mixed with the high-pitched, staccato screams that had jerked him from sleep were the sounds of hurried shuffling and agitated speech. A few steps took him out the door, past the group gathered at the end of the hall, and into the room.

Although he was without his glasses, he took in what he could of the room: it was almost identical to his own, with a small bed, a chest of drawers, and a desk. What had caused the maid's screams and the interest of the small crowd, however, was the presence of a body sprawled across the bed. Ignoring the hotel manager, who was wailing in French, Dinkins felt the wrist of the corpse. Yes, it was indeed a corpse—the hotel room belonged to the short, dumpy woman, and so did the body.

Inspector Dinkins turned to the assembled group. The man of the green suit, now in pajamas, was supporting the plump woman, who had, it appeared, been overcome by the excitement; the American and the young lady were both chattering excitedly; surrounding these were a row of maids and the aproned cook, who wore a paralyzed expression of horror. They were all surprised by the sudden change in Joseph Dinkins.

His eyes were steely; his mouth, set and determined; every muscle in his body held a new tension and purpose. "All right, all right. Everyone out!" he commanded. Greeted by a loud French protest, he turned to face the manager. "You too, LeClair," he said firmly. "Go and call the local police."

The small man's face visibly crumpled. "But, monsieur," he cried, his voice thick with accent and emotion, "do you not see? My reputation! Oh, mon Dieu! No one will want to stay in this hotel . . . my downfall! C'est fini, monsieur!"

Dinkins took him by the shoulders. "LeClair," he said, "there will be a much bigger mess if you don't hop along now and call the police. Go!"

LeClair walked sadly from the room, turning only once to look back at Dinkins. "If I may be so bold, monsieur . . ."

"Yes?"

"Who are you?"

"I'm Inspector Joseph Dinkins of Scotland Yard," said he proudly. "And I mean to solve this case before my car gets back from that confounded auto mechanic!"

In less than one hour, the hotel was swarming with forensic technicians and blue-suited bobbies, all of them examining the rooms, collecting samples of dried blood from the coverlet, and covering almost everything suspicious in a thin layer of dust. "To look for fingerprints, miss," they would explain in an important manner when questioned by an inquisitive and admiring maid. And whenever "something of interest" was discovered, one of them would report excitedly to Room 12, where Dinkins and two fellow inspectors sat tapping their pencils against their teeth and exploring every

corner of the case. And whenever "a detail of impor-
tance" needed to be known, one of the three would
march out of the room to find the desired person and
say something ominous, like "Your presence is required
in the interrogation room, please," and the victim would
be led off with chattering teeth.

By the end of the morning, Dinkins, Burns, and
Robertson had received several black stares from Le-
Clair, drunk many cups of black coffee, and amassed
a considerable amount of information. They learned
that the murdered woman was called Mrs. Maria Humphries and had lived in a small flat in London with her
husband, who had been properly shocked and crushed
by the news. She was fifty-seven; she and her husband
had been born in Rumford and moved away after the
marriage; she had come back to visit her mother. Her
father had died of kidney failure several months ago.
That was all Mr. Humphries, in his upset state, could
tell them. From the mother, who also lived in a small
flat and consequently had no room for her daughter
to stay (hence the hotel), they only learned that Mrs.
Humphries had left her yesterday at teatime in a fine
mood. Did she always act so fidgety and nervous? Oh
yes (a fit of sobs at the other end of the line), it was
her nature; but, no, she couldn't explain a sudden faint-
ing fit.

The three inspectors had also interviewed each oc-
cupant of the hotel. All had given their names and addresses, and none had a suitable alibi, unless deep sleep
could be counted as a defense. The American was named
James Herbert. He was from New York and was in
Rumford on vacation. ("Funny spot for a vacation,"
Robertson had observed—but no one could see a pos-

sible connection between a robust American and a dead London woman.) Did he know Mrs. Humphries? "Of course not," he replied, and then, with a fierce look in his eye, "anyway, what are you trying to imply? Always picking on the American, aren't you? Well, let me tell you something, buddy . . ." At which point James Herbert was discreetly ushered from the room.

The other man, who had by now donned his green suit once more, was from Rumford and had the unfortunate name of Maxwell Jujubie. ("Good God, where did he get a name like that?" Burns had wondered. "Sounds like an alias to me," the suspicious Robertson had said.) He was at the hotel because he was having extermination done at his house. "Damned unpleasant," he muttered in explanation, "but if you knew my sister . . ." The young woman, as it turned out, was his daughter and named Elizabeth. All three inspectors, as it turned out, shared Dinkins's views on her legs, but unfortunately Mr. Jujubie requested that she not be interviewed. "Only thirteen, after all."

Finally, they interviewed the plump woman. Her name was Ms. Jenkins. Married? No. She, like Mrs. Humphries, had grown up in Rumford and moved away at twenty-five. Her husband had recently died, and she was moving back to be near her family, and was looking for a smaller house.

The three men now sat staring at the sheets of names and addresses, feeling the effects of too much coffee and too little breakfast, and tried to discuss the matter in a logical way. Their minds tossed and turned, and turned and tossed, but they were unsuccessful in their efforts. Robertson wanted to arrest everyone, Dinkins was running out of possibilities, and Burns kept saying, "Good God, men, why can't we break and take a proper lunch? I'm about starving—only had one crumpet, I did, only one crumpet."

It was after about half an hour of this type of futile talk that the three men decided that the only productive thing to do would be to follow Burns's suggestion—to have a nice hot lunch and maybe a nap. The hotel, however, was in disorder as they wandered through the kitchen and restaurant in search of the cook. Entering the Red Lounge, they found him commiserating with the entire group and a weepy, matronly woman in a heavy black veil draped comically over one eye.

Mrs. Anna Smith, as she declared herself to be, wished to speak to the inspectors, make sure everything was being done properly, and collect her daughter's things. Robertson took her firmly by the arm and was leading her out when she stopped abruptly and stiffened like a distracted dog on a leash, digging her heels into the floor and leaning forward. "Janet?" was her incredulous whisper.

The air in the Red Lounge was stuffy and tense. The four hotel guests, who had been detained all day, were strained at every nerve by the three inquisitors, the continuous running about of bobbies, and the suspicious stares that had been shot from one person to another as they passed in the hallway or looked up from their books. Dinkins, Burns, and Robertson, on the other hand, were filled with a sudden and unexpected glimmer of excitement which had sprung from hopeless despair. The maids, who had been shaken by this departure from their routine of dusting and wiping, were curious and confused. All in all, not an eye wandered from the old woman as she gazed across the room.

Mrs. Smith dropped her handbag, pointed, and sank into the closest chair with a squeak. "Janet," she repeated. "Whatever are you doing here?"

One of the maids took a step back.

Dinkins kneeled down to face the old woman. "How do you know this person?" he asked hopefully.

She spit the words out like bad nuts. "Janet was my daughter's friend, back when Janet was going about with George. George took quite a fancy to Maria, after a while." She went on with almost gleeful anger. "They married, they did, and Janet decided to show herself in her true colors. A more ill-adjusted one I never saw. Wailing at first, then bitter and vicious. She told Maria"—the old woman pushed herself to her feet once more—"she told Maria, when George and Maria were moving away to London, she told her that if she ever set eyes on her again, she would kill her!"

The words hung frozen in the air; no one moved except the single maid. She advanced to face her accuser. Dinkins could almost feel her pulsating anger as she stood tall, stiff, and terrible in the center of the room, her formerly meek eyes blazing and her fingers twitching convulsively. "You old witch," she sputtered. "You always hated me, you did . . . you and that little thieving daughter o' yours. And you know I didn't do it. You know I could never actually kill her, much as I wished to, much as I thought about it. And these, these here detective blokes, they won't listen to rot like yours. They'll find out. They'll find out it wasn't me." And she collapsed onto the rug in a fit of exhausted tears.

"Well," remarked Joseph Dinkins after some minutes, "it appears that we've made progress."

Inspector Griggs harrumphed quietly. "Sir?"

Looking up, Dinkins realized that poor Griggs had been too polite to do anything but sit quietly while every detail of the case was being remembered on the other side of the desk. "Well, I am sorry, my good man. Dashed beastly of me; go on, please."

Griggs, relieved, sat up a little straighter before starting to talk. "I've reviewed the case, sir. Now, according to the notes, a Mrs. Anna Smith, the dead woman's mother, identified Janet Dillard as an enemy of her daughter. Dillard was convicted, using that association and some other evidence . . ."

"Ah yes," recalled Dinkins, "that handkerchief. And the cigarette ash. Stupid woman, to walk around smoking such a damned rare cigarette—but it was rather obvious once we remembered she'd been in the room when Humphries fainted."

"Yes, sir. And was soon executed as judged. But, sir, here's the problem. Recently, a Mr. George Humphries—the victim's husband, sir—passed away."

"Oh, really?" murmured Dinkins. "That's quite sad. But I don't see what it has to do with—"

Poor Griggs had had about enough. With a pained look at the Chief Inspector, he said patiently, "Well, sir, as I was about to say . . ."

"Oh. Sorry."

"Yes, sir. As I was about to say, some of 'is correspondence was found by 'is mother, sir, and she had a quick look through, like. And she found a letter from his wife, sir, dated ten years before 'er death."

Dinkins sat forward.

Griggs continued. "The content of the letter was alarming, sir, and quite disturbing. It was a complicated story. She started out by saying that she'd sinned long ago and carried the burden of guilt around with her for a long time, but felt that now that they were married—she and 'umphries, that is—she felt she ought to tell 'im."

"Burden of guilt?"

"Or some such emotional babble, sir. The letter goes on to say that this incident took place while Mrs. 'umphries (or Ms. Smith, as she was then called) was working as a sort of child-minder for someone in the town. There was a robbery at the house. Quite a big deal, it was—brought in all the police. Even an inspector from Scotland Yard."

Beads of sweat were standing out on Dinkins's brow.

"At the time, Ms. Smith was quite poor. What with that and some other pieces of circumstantial evidence, she was one of the primary suspects. The inspector on the case knew that, too, and was all ready to drag her in on charges. O' course the case, as I said, sir, was purely circumstantial. If Ms. Smith had had the wits to sit tight, she would have been fine. But she was a young woman, just out of school, and fairly flighty, and she didn't want her father, who was sick at the time, to have any stress."

Dinkins thought that he might like a cup of strong coffee.

"So, as the young inspector was a malleable one, she decided—and rather unwisely, sir—on a course of action. She bribed him. Took one hundred pounds or so out of her savings and gave it to him. He accepted the bribe and brought some crazy story back to Scotland Yard, so as to keep her out of trouble, sir. But he told her that if ever she tried to find him again or to use the information against him, he would kill her." Here Griggs paused to refold his long, gangly legs and to look at his watch. "Apparently she found some new information just before the letter was written. Told her husband in the letter that she'd found it back then, when the case was still pending. She was askin' 'im whether she'd better bring it to the attention of the police."

"Did she?"

"Yes, she did, sir. The letter said that she came in an' told an inspector who was working at a desk. But apparently he didn't quite believe her straight off, sir, and since she was a little nervous about the whole thing, she excused herself and left. The worker at the desk probably thought she was a nut. And, I suppose, it's all for the better that she didn't tell the whole story, tell how she bribed the inspector back in 1904. Except . . ." His voice trailed off.

Dinkins was now leaning toward the speaker, his hands wrapped around the shiny wood of the desk. "Except what, Griggs? Except what?"

"Well, this woman had nothing to hide, but, in a way, she was in danger. The inspector that she bribed probably thought that Maria 'umphries wouldn't try to find him, since she had as much to hide as he did. But what if he heard about her new findings some-how, from the other inspector at the desk? Then he would know, wouldn't he, that she could prove her-self innocent and therefore was free to go after him.

Blackmail him, reveal the facts to the public, whatever she liked. This unknown inspector could have quit or moved away long ago, yes. But, on the other hand, he could still have been working. Still working away at Scotland Yard, working in a sturdy career, sir. And if he were to think that Maria 'umphries was trying to find him again, to blackmail him, he would be ready to take the action he threatened so long ago."

Dinkins leaned back in the chair, blew out a mouthful of air, and took in another one, quickly, nervously. "Was that all the letter said?"

"No, sir. There was one more thing. She mentioned his name."

A telephone rang in the outside office, but neither man heard it.

"His . . . name?"

Griggs rose to his feet. "I 'ave the letter here, sir. But I don't think you need to see it. I think you know the name. I think you know it quite well."

The Chief Inspector of Scotland Yard's face was suddenly drained of blood.

"My question, sir," said Inspector Griggs, "is this: In the Rumford Inn, was it Janet Dillard whom Mrs. 'umphries recognized? Or did she see someone else? Was there another familiar face in the room? Another person—a Scotland Yard official who also recognized her as a danger to him?"

Dinkins opened his dry mouth and shut it again. The feeling of power and prestige that his title gave him had been stripped away in less than five minutes, and he could see the future as though through a window. A humiliating stay in jail, a revealing trial; first his honor, then his job, then his life would be taken.

He tried to stare the young man down, but any eyes can bore into a guilty conscience suddenly reawakened. "Damn!" was all he said. He damned himself, damned himself for the careful process of forgetting he'd put himself through these last twenty years. He'd thought he was safe—stupid thing! Now Griggs knew, and soon everyone would know, and they'd find out how he'd stolen the handkerchief and the cigarette and crept through the hallway in the dead of night with the knife in his hand. That stupid Maria Humphries! That stupid letter! It ruined him. All in five minutes. Five minutes that were the result of thirty years.

Inspector Griggs, meanwhile, gave a nervous cough. He had just realized that he was in a small room with a killer, who very possibly might have a gun around. He didn't particularly want to be shot—he liked life all right and, for another thing, was due in one hour to meet a certain Natasha Batanov for lunch in a dimly lit hotel. So he coughed again and hoped the ordeal would soon be over.

That second cough changed Dinkins's life. It caused him to wake from his black reverie and remember how confused and temptable he had been as a young officer. He saw a way out: he saw a way back to his comfortable life of hot baths and good cheese and nice port. He leaned over the desk and, in as sugary and seductive a voice that ever a fifty-year-old man has mustered, said, "Come on, Griggs. Let's see if we can find a compromise here, eh? A little compromise between two clever men?"

The young Inspector Griggs paused. He thought of Natasha Batanov, who was no doubt used to Hungarian noblemen with healthy bank accounts; he thought of his small, cramped apartment and cheap car. He could use some help, he thought.

"Well?" said the Chief Inspector, tauntingly.

"How much?" asked Griggs.

ABOUT THE AUTHOR

Katherine Stanley lives in Dunbarton, New Hampshire, and is a student at Derryfield School in Manchester. She plays the viola in an orchestra and in quartets and says she is always singing or whistling. Katherine has performed in several musicals and likes following political and environmental issues. Soccer, basketball, and lacrosse are her favorite sports.

Bradley was richer, Bradley
was smarter, and Bradley was a liar.

Theft

by ELIZABETH WEBSTER

I looked up at Mr. Rodriguez in disbelief.

"*D–?*" I asked. He fumbled with his marking book.

"Yes, *D–.*" He closed the book and looked up at me. *Advice time*, I thought. I knew this ritual only too well. He flung the navy book onto his mahogany desk and stood up. I'd never noticed how big he was before. "Now, I suggest this to you, young man: Stop cutting class, do your homework, and . . . for God's sake, boy," he slammed his hand down on my shoulder, "look at me when I talk to you!"

Our eyes met. It wasn't exactly pleasant. His eyebrows were all scrunched together and he looked about ready to howl. Truth was, I felt like picking up the ceramic map of Spain he had on his desk and . . . well, you can imagine what.

I left school that day in one of the worst moods of my entire life. Besides trying to figure out a way of explaining how I managed to get below my usual *D* in Spanish, I had Bradley English, "the mama's boy," walking me home. He lived in one of those rich, three-story houses—you know, the kind with an attic so big you can fit a whole apartment into it.

I looked at my feet. They didn't offer much consolation. I trudged through the snow and ice in my worn-out Nikes. They had little holes all over the place, and my feet were becoming painfully numb because the sneakers seemed to be absorbing more water than they were repelling.

I looked over at Brad. He looked like a big, fat stuffed animal, wearing tons and tons of woolen articles and a down jacket that must have taken five hundred ducks to stuff. His combat boots clunked against the cement sidewalk and made my feet feel even colder.

I opened my new pack of Newport Lights and lit one up in an attempt to get the jerk off my trail. He hurried after me still. "You know," he began, "you really shouldn't smoke so much. Studies have shown that it can damage your lungs." I kept my eyes glued straight ahead, keeping my mouth shut. I thought to myself: *What I wouldn't do for that ceramic map now!*

"Listen," he continued. "I'm not trying to pester you. I'm simply stating the statistics." He put his hand on my shoulder to slow me down. This was too much.

I turned to him. "*You* listen," I began. "Why doesn't pwecious wittle Bwadley skip on home to his mommy? Hurry along now! She might get worried that her pumpkin got hurt or something . . . and wittle Bwadley wouldn't want his mommy to worry now, would he?" With this, I let a mouthful of smoke out into his fat face. I can be pretty nasty sometimes, if I'm in the mood. He coughed for a minute or so and then let the subject drop. I always knew he was a smart boy.

I turned down Avenue I. *Two more blocks to go,* I thought to myself. *Thank God for that.* I glanced around the neighborhood . . . my neighborhood. After last night's snowstorm it had become almost unrecognizable. Thick blankets of snow covered the cars of those smart enough to stay home, and white frost lined the tiny barren branches of trees, making them look glossy and delicate. Besides my numb body, and having to trudge in snow that came way above my ankles, I loved the winter. It made everything so peaceful.

Suddenly a little squirt in a leather jacket tore through me and Brad, ramming my arm into my stomach. The kid knocked Brad down to the cement, where his heavy body landed with a *thunk* in a large frozen puddle. I looked up. The kid had a pocketbook. Then I heard the scream.

It was from Mrs. Rutherford, the widow who lived in the apartment two doors down from mine. "Help! Help!" she screeched. "Hoodlum! Hoodlum! Come back here, you—"

It didn't take me long to figure out what was going on, and it didn't take Mrs. Rutherford long to realize that Brad and I were the only ones to help. I looked up at her, and her eyes pierced my very soul. She turned away.

"Brad! Bradley English! Help! Help!" She never did like me. Nevertheless, I knew that stuffed excuse for a boy wouldn't do anything. I had to do something, whether she trusted me or not.

I dropped my books on Brad and ran after the boy. My sneakers didn't provide the best traction in the world, and I was surprised that I didn't go flying into a fence or something.

As soon as Mrs. Rutherford realized that I was the one doing the running, her shrieks became more and more horror-filled. I heard her bang Brad on the head with her umbrella and tell him to get off his rear and get her purse. His slow and heavy footsteps followed after me. I could tell he was more than a little reluctant.

The kid I was chasing was pretty small, and finally I caught up with him. He had on a torn brown leather jacket and was wearing sneakers, like me. I could hear him breathing heavily. When I got to within two or three feet of him, I gave a flying leap and landed on the kid's back. We hit some smooth ice and went sliding for about two car-lengths. Finally we stopped moving. I just lay there—on top of his back. I was pretty big for my age and the kid couldn't budge. He began to whimper.

I brought my rough hands up to his neck and picked him up by his torn collar. His face was red, and he refused to look me in the eye. I grabbed the pocketbook from his grip. It didn't take much effort—the kid was pretty weak.

Just then, Brad came puffing up the block. His warm breath came out in blasts, and huge clouds of white formed before his face. He wobbled over and stood beside me. I couldn't think with him there, as usual. "Here," I said, and I slapped the purse into his hand. He looked at me with this confused look on his fat face. For the life of him, he couldn't figure out what to do with it. I slapped him upside his head and shoved him in the direction of Mrs. Rutherford. He nodded and was off, walking slower than my mom drives in the snow.

I turned back to the kid. He just stood there, not even attempting to move. It was as if he almost wanted to be caught. I gripped my hands around his scrawny white neck and put my face in his. He was only nine or ten. His hair was dirty blond, not really knotted or anything, but kind of filthy looking—and feeling. His pale white skin was stained with streaks of black muck or something, and he didn't smell good. No, he didn't smell good at all. He didn't look good at all. He looked like a kid who had no one to look out for him, no one to love him. That made me hesitate before closing my hand harder around his neck. I could empathize with him. But that didn't make what he did right.

I pulled myself together and grasped his head—this no-eye-contact bit was getting to me. With a jerk of the head, his eyes met mine. He had glossy gray eyes with a trace of blue in them. But the blue seemed to have been strained out of them, leaving them drab and icy. Icy and so very distant. They looked at me in such a way that I almost let go of him. But I couldn't. I had to say something.

"Now tell me, kid," I began, "what's your name?" He struggled to get away but, as I said, he was pretty weak. He didn't get anywhere.

"I ain't got no name," he spit out. I took hold of his arm.

"Well," I began, "whatever you want to call yourself . . . is this your idea of fun—stealing little old ladies' purses? Huh?" I swung him around and pushed his scrawny body against a blue van. He was really tiny! And he looked so afraid—so pitiful! I tried to appear furious. "Now listen here, kid! How would you like it if I went and told your mom and pop about this little hobby of yours? Hmmm? You wouldn't like it too much, would you?"

He looked down at his frayed jeans and bit his lip. By this time I had stopped pushing him against the van. Now he was just standing there in front of me. All of a sudden he had this funny expression on his face—one that I couldn't quite make out. Finally he spoke.

"I ain't got no old man," he said in barely a whisper, "and no mother, either. So take me to the police if ya feel like it, 'cause I could care less!"

My hand loosened its grip around his neck and my fingers didn't push into his jacket so hard. Suddenly I knew why he was so weak! So could he help it if his parents went and died on him? Suddenly I didn't see him as a criminal. I saw him as a little kid who just wanted some spare change for maybe a bite to eat. And I wanted to help.

I stuck my hand into my jacket pocket and pulled out the three bucks I had made last week shoveling walks. I was gonna use them to buy myself a pair of gloves down at the A&P. Oh well, my hands were used to being cold anyway.

I pushed the money into his coat pocket and looked him in the eye. "Listen, kid—don't go around stealing old ladies' purses . . . or anyone's. Or wallets or watches or jewelry, hear? It ain't right. It just ain't." I patted the money in his tattered pocket. "Now move along and get yourself something to eat at the store. And no candy. Eat some meat or something, got it?"

He looked at me as if he were about to cry and

nodded his head. I was probably the first person who had cared for him in years. He straightened up, and that caring look faded from his eyes. For someone who has never been loved, it is hard to love.

I gulped to hold back what was coming. "Now get lost." I stepped back and watched him tear out of sight, in the direction of Martha's Deli and Hero Shop.

When he was no more than a tiny speck in the distance, I looked down at the gray pavement. It was rough and uneven, broken to small pieces in places. " . . . unfair," I said aloud, half not hearing my own voice. "Why? Why?"

For the life of me, I couldn't understand why this poor kid was deprived of his parents and why Brad had . . . well, just about everything. Funny I had never noticed how unfair life was before. I always just accepted that Brad's parents had one of those big, black, shiny cars and mine got stuck with a little silver Toyota Tercel with a broken headlight and stolen radio. And everyone liked him, trusted him. Well, what about me? Why didn't they like me? And who was the one to get Mrs. Rutherford's pocket—my thoughts were cut off by the reminder of what had just happened. The pocketbook! I had forgotten all about it. I turned around and started toward 36th Street, where the kid had bumped into me and Brad.

Mrs. Rutherford was standing with her pocketbook in hand and a large grin on her wrinkled face. Her lips rolled back to reveal a ton of gum and two large gold caps. They sparkled under the glare of the sun and somehow gave off a warning signal that said, "Stay away, kid."

I started to think of possible excuses as to how the

kid got away. I couldn't explain what happened—they wouldn't understand. I decided to say he was too quick for me. "You see, Mrs. Rutherford," I would say, "the kid was just too quick for me. Every time I tried to grab him, he would slip right out from under me. Oh, well. At least I got you your pocketbook back—that's what really counts." Then she'd smile at me and get all mushy—thanking me left and right—and I would smile back at her and tell her it was nothing, nothing at all. I decided that she wouldn't care much if the kid got away. At least I hoped she wouldn't.

When I was a block away from them, I looked up. Brad was telling some kind of story. As I came closer, I could pick up a few of his words. Here's what he was saying:

"You see, Mrs. Rutherford, he was tough, but I could handle him . . ."

I couldn't believe what I was hearing! I really couldn't. He continued.

"Yes, it was dangerous . . . but with my fighting experience it was no trouble at all . . . could've done it with one hand tied behind my back."

He was dishing it out!

"With his fighting experience?" I nearly screamed. The thought of it made me laugh. She couldn't buy it . . . she wouldn't buy it.

Brad saw me coming and gulped. He bent over and lifted his books off the snow-covered cement, never taking his eyes from the sidewalk.

I turned to Mrs. Rutherford and cleared my throat. "Um . . ." I began. "I . . . ah . . . see you've got your pocketbook, ma'am."

She turned a cold eye on me. "It's Mrs. Rutherford

to you, young man," she said abruptly. "And, yes, I did get my pocketbook. Bradley here got it for me." She turned around and looked with kindly eyes upon the stuffed duck.

I was beginning to feel ill . . . and kind of dizzy. I couldn't accept what was happening. I really couldn't. But at least she didn't ask where the kid was. That was something . . . I guess.

"Yes," she continued, "you could do worse than to take a few lessons from this young man." With this, she patted him on the shoulder. I caught a glimpse of his dark brown, almost black eyes. They were kind of glazed, and they looked a little scared. He smiled politely and then spoke up.

"Well, ah . . . ma'am," he began. "It was no trouble, no trouble at all." He was backing up the sidewalk. If he didn't watch it, he'd fall out over the curb. "No trouble," he repeated. He cleared his throat. "But I'll have to . . . ah . . . get going. Gotta get home. You know how Mother worries when I'm out late—and in the snow? Whew! Would she be upset! Ah . . . yeah, well—bye, Mrs. Rutherford. Bye, um . . ." He looked up at me. "Bye." The coward couldn't even say my name. I looked into his ruddy face. My eyes hit his and I must have been giving him the dirtiest look ever, 'cause he just turned around and practically raced up the street—almost got hit by a station wagon crossing Brooklyn Avenue.

By this time I had given up. Everyone always thought I was a loser . . . why should now be any different? It wasn't. It would never be different.

Out of nowhere it began to flurry. I really didn't understand that—it was sunny a minute ago. The cold

flakes fell on my nose and my numb fingers and re-
minded me again of how cold I was—just what I needed.

Mrs. Rutherford looked over at me. "What's the
matter with you, boy?" she said. "Where are your
gloves . . . and your hat?" Her eyebrows slowly lowered. "For God's sake, doesn't your mother take care
of you?"

That stung. I kept my eyes on the ground, staring,
going over the tiny cracks in the pavement. I had never
noticed how badly the sidewalks around here needed
repair. Mrs. Rutherford just stood there, probably staring at me. People are always staring at me for one reason or another.

"Well, boy," she continued, "thanks for helping
Bradley get my pocketbook. I'll be on my way now."
She stood there. She must have expected me to respond with a "you're welcome" or even a simple "good-
bye," but I just didn't feel like saying anything. She'd
have to wait there all day and night if she wanted something outta me. She mumbled something I didn't quite
catch and was finally on her way.

It began to snow harder, and my ears and cheeks
felt as if they really weren't on my face. I kept biting
my lip and I had this funny feeling in my throat—kind
of like I was about to cry. I had to bite it harder and
harder to keep it all inside, but I couldn't. I guess I
had just had enough. I didn't realize how hard I was
biting my lip until I felt the warm blood stream into
my mouth. My lip began to sting and my teeth lifted
up from it. As I did this, one teardrop rolled out of
the corner of my eye and plopped down on the broken pavement below. It fell between one of the larger
cracks, and the soil soaked it right up.

ABOUT THE AUTHOR

Elizabeth Webster lives in Brooklyn, New York, where she attends Polytechnic Preparatory Country Day School. Besides writing, her interests include singing, acting, playing the piano, and animals. She takes care of six cats, some birds, and two dogs.

Story Index
By genre, topic, and for use as writing models

By Genre

Fantasy/Myth
Beneath a Dark Mountain, 25
In Defense of Hades, 53
The Questing Beast, 73
Starry Night, 107

Historical Fiction
Starry Night, 107

Humor
The Clubhouse, 13
A Day at the Mall, 43
The Mission, 63
The Questing Beast, 73

Mystery
The Chief Inspector, 115

Realistic Fiction
The Clubhouse, 13
Cricket Song, 19
A Day at the Mall, 43
My Father, 47
The Mission, 63
It Rained for Stevie, 93
The Chief Inspector, 115
Theft, 131

By Topic

Childhood
The Clubhouse, 13
The Mission, 63

Coming of Age
The Clubhouse, 13
Beneath a Dark Mountain, 25
My Father, 47
In Defense of Hades, 53
Theft, 131

Community
Cricket Song, 19
Beneath a Dark Mountain, 25

Family
My Father, 47
In Defense of Hades, 53

Freedom/Choice
Cricket Song, 19
Beneath a Dark Mountain, 25
In Defense of Hades, 53
The Mission, 63
Starry Night, 107

Friendship
The Clubhouse, 13
A Day at the Mall, 43
The Mission, 63
The Questing Beast, 73
It Rained for Stevie, 93

The Hero
Beneath a Dark Mountain, 25
My Father, 47
The Questing Beast, 73
Theft, 131

Life & Death
My Father, 47
It Rained for Stevie, 93
Starry Night, 107

Outsiders
Cricket Song, 19
In Defense of Hades, 53
Starry Night, 107
Theft, 131

Teens vs. Family
Beneath a Dark Mountain, 25
My Father, 47
In Defense of Hades, 53